TREASON 2   1

TREASON
TWO
Control Your Urges. Control The Flesh.

T. STYLES

By T. Styles

ARE YOU ON OUR EMAIL LIST?
SIGN UP ON OUR WEBSITE
www.thecartelpublications.com
OR TEXT THE WORD: CARTELBOOKS TO
22828
FOR PRIZES, CONTESTS, ETC.

SHYT LIST 1: BE CAREFUL WHO YOU CROSS
SHYT LIST 2: LOOSE CANNON
SHYT LIST 3: AND A CHILD SHALL LEAVE THEM
SHYT LIST 4: CHILDREN OF THE WRONGED
SHYT LIST 5: SMOKIN' CRAZIES THE FINALE'
PITBULLS IN A SKIRT 1
PITBULLS IN A SKIRT 2
PITBULLS IN A SKIRT 3: THE RISE OF LIL C
PITBULLS IN A SKIRT 4: KILLER KLAN
PITBULLS IN A SKIRT 5: THE FALL FROM GRACE
POISON 1
POISON 2
VICTORIA'S SECRET
HELL RAZOR HONEYS 1
HELL RAZOR HONEYS 2
BLACK AND UGLY
BLACK AND UGLY AS EVER
MISS WAYNE & THE QUEENS OF DC
BLACK AND THE UGLIEST
A HUSTLER'S SON
A HUSTLER'S SON 2
THE FACE THAT LAUNCHED A THOUSAND BULLETS
YEAR OF THE CRACKMOM
THE UNUSUAL SUSPECTS
LA FAMILIA DIVIDED
RAUNCHY
RAUNCHY 2: MAD'S LOVE
RAUNCHY 3: JAYDEN'S PASSION
MAD MAXXX: CHILDREN OF THE CATACOMBS (EXTRA RAUNCHY)
KALI: RAUNCHY RELIVED: THE MILLER FAMILY
REVERSED
QUITA'S DAYSCARE CENTER
QUITA'S DAYSCARE CENTER 2
DEAD HEADS
DRUNK & HOT GIRLS
PRETTY KINGS
PRETTY KINGS 2: SCARLETT'S FEVER
PRETTY KINGS 3: DENIM'S BLUES
PRETTY KINGS 4: RACE'S RAGE
HERSBAND MATERIAL
UPSCALE KITTENS
WAKE & BAKE BOYS
YOUNG & DUMB
YOUNG & DUMB: VYCE'S GETBACK
TRANNY 911
TRANNY 911: DIXIE'S RISE
FIRST COMES LOVE, THEN COMES MURDER
LUXURY TAX
THE LYING KING
CRAZY KIND OF LOVE
SILENCE OF THE NINE
SILENCE OF THE NINE II: LET THERE BE BLOOD
SILENCE OF THE NINE III

4

By T. Styles

WWW.THECARTELPUBLICATIONS.COM

TREASON 2

Control Your Urges Control

The Flesh

By

T. STYLES

Library of Congress Control Number:

ISBN 10: 1948373785

ISBN 13: 978-1948373784

Cover Design: Book Slut Girl

First Edition

Printed in the United States of America

What Up Fam,

I'm not even gonna hold you too long because I want you to jump into this new world that T. Styles has immersed us in, but I do want to say something...

Please be kind to one another! Folks so worried about cancelling folks and being about the 'cancel culture' that they forget to be human. Remember to be human, have compassion and empathy for one another. Put love and kindness first. Please.

Now...TREASON 2! I know y'all didn't see TREASON coming but once T pulled you in, she had you and part 2 will really delve deeper into these Vamp and Wolf worlds! You will not be able to put it down until it's over so clear your calendar and grab your drinks and snacks! You in for an amazing ride!

With that being said, keeping in line with tradition, we want to give respect to a vet, new trailblazer paving the way or pay homage to a favorite. In this novel, we would like to recognize:

Michael K. Williams

Michael Kenneth Williams was an AMAZING, AMAZING Emmy nominated actor! His body of work in film and TV is crazy! I will not be able to list them all in this love note, but here are a few standout performances including one of my ALL-TIME favorite TV shows, The Wire! As well as, Boardwalk Empire, Hap & Leonard, The Night Of, Lackawanna Blues, When They See Us, Community and Lovecraft Country. Trust me, he was supremely talented and if

8   By T. Styles

you have not checked out his work, please do yourself a favor and indulge!
May he forever rest in peace.

Ok fam...get into it! I'll see you in the next novel!

Love y'all and God Bless!

Charisse "C. Wash" Washington
Vice President
The Cartel Publications
www.thecartelpublications.com
www.facebook.com/publishercwash
Instagram: publishercwash
www.twitter.com/cartelbooks
www.facebook.com/cartelpublications
www.theelitewritersacademy.com
Follow us on Instagram: Cartelpublications

#CartelPublications
#UrbanFiction
#PrayForCece
#RIPMichaelKWilliams

#TREASON2

By T. Styles

"If I tell you I crave you and that I long to taste you, would you fear me? Because it's true. And so, I ask, what greater love is there than that?"

- **Rue**

PRESENT DAY
"My Sweet Violet."

She wanted to touch him, but the fear of rejection handcuffed her moves.

As soft rain splattered on the chauffeured blood red S class Mercedes Benz. Pierre and Violet sat in the backseat, each in mental universes of their own.

His coolness drove Violet insane. Although she would take nothing from the gentleman manner he appeared to possess, she would love for him to yank her closer, on some hood nigga shit.

Because she would've given herself freely at that moment had he asked. But his vibe made her feel like he didn't care.

Besides, he was on a phone call and despite sitting next to him as he was engrossed in conversation, she didn't hear a word he was saying.

Who was on the call and more important to her at that moment?

And yet, it was dumb to even question him.

They met less than two hours earlier at a coffee shop.

Virtually strangers.

That didn't stop her from going with him. After she learned that her grandmother was dying and that she charged her with finishing up her award-winning book series, her world was crushed.

The next thing she knew, his fine ass walked inside, shared with her his story, and invited her on a date.

Easy, Violet. She told herself. *Don't push him away like all the rest.*

By T. Styles

Instead, she examined him fully, doing her level best to resist the urge to touch him.

To smell him.

Taste him.

Unlike her sisters Chloe and Jeanette, slut wasn't her brand and so she sat patiently for him to finish his call.

But she was growing antsy.

Like a child she resorted to sighing deeply and crossing her legs while running her unmanicured hands up and down her thighs. She even tugged at the bottom of her shirt, pulled up and wiped her dry forehead, which essentially flashed her boobs.

He ain't see none of that shit.

If she wanted the man, she had to cut the games and *say so*.

When he was done, tucking the cell back into his pocket, he sat back, sighed softly, and looked over at her cute face. "What's on your mind my sweet, Violet?"

If he saw the freakshow she just put on he would know she wanted her back banged out. But that was the past.

"I love that," she said.

He wiped a strand of hair behind her ear. His warm knuckles brushed softly against her cheek. "What's that?"

"Everything about you."

He chuckled once. And for some reason, that was enough.

"Who are you?" She asked, digging deeper.

"I've told you more than I have ever told a soul in my life." He positioned his body to see her fully. "Do you still feel like you don't know me enough to enjoy my company tonight?"

Nah, she was going to roll regardless.

In fact, if she could have created the perfect man, he would be it. But she wasn't used to a man not wanting to be sexual with her directly after getting her number, and so, since that didn't appear to be his motive, she felt insecure.

"I just want to know more." She batted her eyes.

"Nah, it's your turn. So, tell me...who are you?"

His eyes stabbed into her soul as he waited for her response.

His attention suddenly had her feeling stupid. If she wanted to talk it appeared he was game. So why was she having trouble coming up with something to say?

"O...okay. What do you wanna know about me?"

"Everything! Don't hold back shit."

She swallowed and quickly searched her mind for a story that could come close to the one he shared with her earlier at the coffee shop. How could she compete with such an amazing tale?

It had all the components necessary for a sweeping drama.

Secrets. Betrayal. Survival. Fear and even incest.

Based on what he said, his mother was raped by her father and as a result, he was the product of electral love. But the tragedy didn't stop there for Pierre.

He and his mother were eventually threatened by the same man, which caused him to run away with the scent of onions on his skin to elude his father/grandfather's vicious dogs.

So, when he asked who she was, in her opinion she was a nobody compared to him.

14   By T. Styles

"Violet...answer me."

A deep breath blasted from her body as she braced herself for his immediate exit. "I'm gullible. A pushover who wants these voices in my mind to stop."

"Voices?"

"They tell me I'm not worthy. They tell me that I will always be used. And they tell me I'm not attractive." She looked to her right out of the window to escape his gaze. "And I listen to them. Because...because--"

She looked downward and he touched her leg. "Why, Violet?"

She smiled and took another deep breath. In her mind it was best to get things over than to prolong the inevitable.

He would leave anyway, right?

"Because of the things I did. Things I felt like I had to do at the time which now seem so wrong. And now I can't take any of them back."

"Do you want to share? I can keep secrets."

She looked at his perfect but slightly scarred face and thought better of it. "I don't wanna go to a restaurant tonight. I'm sorry."

He appeared disappointed.

She liked that. In her warped mind it meant he wanted to keep her longer.

"Sadly, I don't want the night to end. So, where would you like to go? The night is still young my, Sweet Violet."

"Anywhere you are. If you would have me."

Relief overcame him, evident by how relaxed his shoulders appeared.

Five minutes later, they were pulling through his gated property. When the car parked, the driver stepped out and opened their doors.

"I don't usually bring people here." He admitted. "In fact, this is the second time I've done it."

"Why me?" She looked up at him with widened eyes.

"Why not you?"

With a hand to the small of her back, he led her toward the gates of his home. Once the entryway opened, she exhaled as she took in the magnificence of the property. "This...this is..."

Words were unnecessary.

Everything didn't need to be described.

And so, he smiled and guided her further inside until they were in his elaborate living room.

The luxury caused her to stumble.

Oh, so this nigga rich-rich. She thought.

"Who are you? I mean...what do you do for a living?"

He smiled. "Would you like something to drink? Wine? A cocktail? Anything you want I'm sure I have."

The question about what he did for a living was avoided so she would be forced to come up with her own possibilities.

A drug dealer?

A pimp?

A basketball star?

While each of those fields of business may have explained the money, none of them would have explained his swag.

He seemed unreal.

"You choose." She whispered. "I'll drink anything."

16   By T. Styles

Okay, Violet. Get it girl. She thought to herself having liked her response.

He winked and returned moments later with two full wine glasses. Although his drink seemed thicker and redder, she appreciated the beverage's, more than anything, upcoming effects. Because if she were going to relax, she needed a little help.

Sitting next to her, he wrapped his arm behind her which rested on the couch. "I see you, Violet."

She looked away quickly. "What do you see?" She took a large sip. In fact, she drank so much, half the glass was damn near gone.

"I see strength in you." He spoke softly.

She looked at him. "Really?"

"I also see fear. You're afraid of me now. Aren't you?" He continued.

He was right.

Although he had all the looks, he seemed very dark.

Dangerous.

"Should I...should I be?" Her whole body trembled.

"What do you have to look forward to in life?"

"Why?"

"Because I want to be a part of that."

Despite sitting down, she felt like she was falling. This nigga knew exactly what to say.

"My grandmother. She's on my mind."

At that time, she remembered she was in the hospital. Normally thoughts of her Abuela dying consumed every hour in the day. But this man represented a welcomed distraction.

"When she goes, I don't know what I'll do."

"You two are close?"

She shook her head. "That's an understatement, Pierre. She was the only person who got me. Who really understood me." She placed a hand on her chest.

"Was?" He asked.

She made a mistake. Her use of the word *"was"* had her feeling like shit since as of now, her grandmother was not dead.

"I mean...is. I guess I'm bracing for the worst."

"You shouldn't do that." He touched her leg and took a light sip of his drink, which left a thick red stain on his lips. He licked it away.

She wished she could do that for him.

"What kind of woman is your grandmother? I want to know as much as you do."

She giggled. With the exception of the press and her grandmother's fans, no one cared much about Abuela nowadays.

"She's a writer. She wrote Vampire books in a way I've never read before." She giggled. "I think she's the most amazing person I know. I really wish you could meet her."

"Maybe I'll get an opportunity. What's her name?" He moved closer a bit more aggressively than he had in the past and she jumped.

Just a minute ago she would've loved for the man to suck a titty or two but now she was fearful.

Again.

"Why did you...why did you react that way?" He looked her up and down.

"I don't know. I didn't think you were going to rape me or anything like that."

He glared. "After what my mother experienced, with being raped by her own father, that's the one

By T. Styles

thing you can call me that would forever damage how I look at you."

"I'm sorry. I don't consider you a rapist. I misspoke."

"Don't be. Now what's your grandmother's name?"

"I prefer not to tell you that right now. Due to a promise, she made me make about other things."

"Respected," he nodded. "But let me show you why I asked." Softly he grabbed her hand and walked her around the house.

As she took the journey through the massive estate, she breathed in more of his exquisite taste in art and design. Skill was on display in this crib. And if he was responsible for the look and feel of his home, she would consider him a master.

After a storybook trip along elaborate hallways, they approached double doors made of black wood accented with golden knobs. He pushed them open, presenting the most sumptuous library ever imagined.

Flicking on a switch, a soft dim glow filled the space.

Her jaw dropped as she walked slowly inside. "This...this is magnificent."

There were books from the floor to the vaulted ceiling and a rolling ladder that would take a reader in either direction.

"This is where I feel like myself the most." He spoke.

"I don't think I've ever seen these many books before." Violet said as she ran her finger over binder after binder. "They're...they're all so beautiful. Many worlds, etched in time."

"I'm glad you feel me on this my, Sweet Violet. This is my favorite place in the house." He walked to the window and widened the curtains, allowing the moonlight to shine inside.

"What books do you enjoy?" She questioned.

"Mainly nonfiction, but every now and again a classic gets me going too." He paused. "So, when you mentioned your grandmother was a writer, I had to show you."

Maybe there was nothing to fear after all.

It was all so weird. That a man could be both sexy and dark at the same time.

She turned toward him, and he walked over to her. "Wow." She swallowed.

Standing in front of her, he massaged her shoulders lightly. "What is it, Violet?"

She wanted to tell him so many things, even though they just met.

Like how her grandmother wanted her to finish her epic book series, in the event she died. And how she was afraid she wouldn't do her readers justice. Because despite being a fan, she realized her skills were nowhere near what her Abuela possessed.

"As I mentioned lightly, my grandmother's dying. And I discovered that she wants me to do something. Something I'm not ready for."

"What is it?" He stepped even closer, leaving no room between them. "Maybe I can help you. Give me a chance."

He seemed slightly desperate, and she backed away.

This was different from how he acted in the car on the way over when he moved as if she didn't exist.

By T. Styles

"She told me I can't tell anyone. And although I just met you, I want to tell you everything I know and more."

He sighed and she noticed he appeared to exhibit slight rage. Why was he so concerned about her grandmother's books?

"I won't pressure you. Tell me when you're ready." He walked away and Violet took notice.

Had she lost him for good.

"Can I trust you?" She asked.

He paused and faced her.

"With...with everything? Including all of my secrets."

He moved in her direction, but it felt like forever. "You can trust me with anything you say and more. I would never hurt you. I would never betray you." He kissed her gently on the lips. "So what do you want to say?"

CHAPTER ONE
"I can smell you."

Cage Stryker was giving big dick Vampire energy... As the lights hit him and the diamond studded *Magnus* chain around his neck sparkled, he stood in the middle of the private Vampire club like he owned the place. Sipping on something thick, red, and juicy, that came from a cute thick redbone from Southeast D.C., he grinned a little as he understood the change his life had taken.

And since he was amongst his people, he allowed his fangs to remain hung, something most Vamps had no control over, as it happened only whenever they were sexually stimulated, angry or excited.

But at the moment, Cage was simply unflustered.

Feared by some, respected by most just for being Tino's son, many tried to claw into his radar to get his attention.

But he wasn't foolish.

In his opinion there was a blood bounty on his head, courtesy of his former friend Onion and so he had to be careful.

Then again, he always needed to be careful.

But he had some death threats of his own he would see carried out.

After learning that Onion, who was once a friend, killed his father to push Cage deep into the Vampire world, after taking The Fluid, he decided he would get revenge.

In fact, his reason for coming out in public at the moment was all a part of his plan.

To find Onion and to take his life.

By T. Styles

"Sir, Jawan from the Bruckheimer Collection wanted to introduce himself to you," one of his bodyguards said. "If you have the time."

The Bruckheimer Collection had many well-respected Vamps, so Cage nodded to allow him through the red and gold velvet rope.

Model perfect like all of the Vamps in The Collective, not a flaw was in place on his light skin as he approached with respect with two members of his collection at his side.

When he bowed once, Cage shook his hand and waited for his request. "Thank you for seeing me."

"So, you're Jawan." Cage took another sip. "I heard a lot about you."

"Same here," Jawan nodded. "I just wanted to say that whatever you need from me I'm here to help." He turned around and looked at one of his men who held a beautiful gold jug. "This is imported blood from Sierra Leone. It's sweet and juicy."

Cage accepted the gift and handed it to one of his bodyguards.

"I 'ppreciate it. And I'll take you up on your offer if need be. Besides, I'm looking to build allies."

"Welcome to The Collective," Jawan said before walking away.

The moment he bopped off, a beautiful day walking Vampire with skin the color of an opal stone approached. "Hello, I'm Carmen and--."

"I saw you when you first walked inside." Cage was shaken by her beauty.

She blushed.

She was fine, but his comment wasn't meant to be personal or flirtatious for that matter. So shawty was doing the most as she whipped her hair over her shoulder and puckered her lips.

He saw everybody when they walked inside or moved in his direction.

"You haven't taken The Fluid." Cage said, raising his chin. "Why?"

"How did you know?" She was shocked at his skill level.

He inhaled deeply. "I can smell you. Now, what you doing in here if you haven't taken The Fluid?"

She frowned. Choosing to ignore him she responded, "But...but Vamps can't smell one another."

He was on a different level and didn't have time to put her on to his game. Besides, it didn't matter anyway.

"What do you want?" He said observing her closely.

"I have the Vampire gene, but I haven't accepted any requests to join a collection. And I was wondering if you would have me. I promise to be a good--."

"I'm not taking on a collection right now," he said, interrupting her.

"Why not? How will you stay protected if--"

"Good night, Carmen. It was nice to meet you."

"Are you dismissing me?"

Silence.

"I think that would be a big mistake." She lowered her brow. "You may be Tino's son, but it's important to remember he's dead now. You need to pick a squad for your own good."

Cage yanked her up. "What you just say to me, bitch?" His neck corded.

From afar many observed. Including his bodyguard who whispered, "Sir, people are watching."

Instead of relenting, he squeezed harder. "What did you just say to me?"

"N...nothing." His strength and developed skill level shocked her, even for a Vamp who had taken The Fluid. "I didn't mean any disrespect." She could barely speak.

Releasing her he said to the bodyguard, "Get her out of here!"

"Sure thing, boss," he responded as he escorted her toward the exit with a set of knuckles to her back shoulder.

As she was pushed away, she looked back once before disappearing from the establishment.

Afterwards, one by one Vamps walked up to Cage, all bearing gifts, mostly of the blood kind.

Despite their generosity Cage had zero intention on drinking any of that shit. Because he knew that very soon, someone would look to make good on a longstanding promise to take his life.

And he was right.

Because in the back of the club Onion stood watching, with nothing but hate, and jealousy in his heart. Disguised a bit ridiculously, he wore a fedora pulled way down over his eyes and was dressed inconspicuously in black slacks, a white t-shirt, and a suit jacket.

If it were true that Cage developed his senses more advanced than most Vamps, Onion knew he had to hang back, or risk Cage picking up his scent.

"You see that nigga fronting like he run shit?" Onion said to Spikes, one of the unruly Vamps who still believed Onion was going to reclaim his spot-on top of The Collective.

"I see him." He glared. "You want me to get at him?"

When he moved to steal Cage in his jaw, Onion tugged at his wrist. "Nah, I know what I gotta do to take him off his throne. And he won't see it coming."

THE NEXT NIGHT
The Stryker Estate
"When will you put me first?"

The black leather curtains darkened the room so much, one could not see their hands before their face.

Cage liked it this way.

Especially when it was time to fuck.

Angelina's body melted under Cage's as he pumped in and out of her warmth. Her sweet fruity odor, coupled with the softness of her body and the tingling sensations in his stiffness caused him to want to lock her away forever.

Just so he could feel the sensation every minute.

And every second of each day.

As she wrapped her warm legs around him, he snaked his hands under her ass and pulled lightly apart.

He was exploring.

Searching.

By T. Styles

For the one place he hadn't been to within her body. They fucked so many times that unfortunately he was coming up short, but it didn't stop him from wanting to go with the flow.

Her pussy felt that good.

Like velvet.

"I love you, Cage," she moaned as she looked into his eyes. "I...I never want this feeling to end."

Her sentiments were sweet.

Truly.

And he enjoyed them every now and again. But at the moment, he wanted this experience to be a bit nasty. He wanted to imagine the vilest acts, as he felt the wetness of her body up under him.

Even though she was his wife.

"Do you love me, Cage?" She moaned. "I want so much to hear you say the words.

Damn she was annoying. He thought.

"You know I do," he continued to pump. "Just...just keep it like that okay?"

"Then let me hear the words."

This wasn't going to work.

He couldn't bust properly if she were going to keep at the emotional games.

Lately Angelina was in what he described as being an over sentimental, sappy mood. And no matter how much he reassured her that his love for her was legit, after all, he made her his wife, she was jealous of his new life.

On the darker side.

And those who threw themselves at his feet simply because he was, "the Vamp future" although she was still unclear on what that meant.

Cage loved her, but the constant need to be validated was weighing on him in a way that he felt was, well, less appealing.

He wanted their marital bond to be the uplift she needed to rise to queen level.

She had yet to make the mark.

"I love you, Angelina," and with that he pounded so hard, her next words couldn't be heard without her teeth chattering together.

He hoped it was good enough to keep her silent.

It was.

His fuck game was spectacular.

Cage knew the body and he understood what was necessary to make her vibrate in ways that could be addictive. If she wasn't his, he may have held back some of his fuck game for fear a lesser woman wouldn't be able to handle it. But he wanted her to feel all of him fully. He wanted the scratches on his back that oozed blood for a moment, only to heal quickly thereafter.

He wanted her to bite into his skin as he longed to bite into hers.

He wanted it all and so he fucked her in a way that couldn't compare to any man before him, including his once good friend Onion.

Actually, that was always his plan.

To be better than the man, who was once his best friend. Since, unfortunately, they both had her.

Once he hit the spot, deep in the back and toward the right, he eased in and out in a way that tickled her clit every time.

And then it happened. Electric pulse like sensations that had them both screaming at the moon.

By T. Styles

"Damn that felt so fucking good." She trembled. "I...I would burn down the world if you left me."

"And I would kill you, if you ever left me," he said staring directly into her eyes, as semen continued to rush from his body.

In the midst of violent threats, they both arrived.

It was good, but they had better.

Was their marriage reaching its end?

Rolling off of her body he kissed her lips, flipped on the light, and looked into her eyes. "Damn...your pussy is still so sweet." He sat on the side of the bed.

"Your fangs," she said pointing at him. "They're down."

"I'm sorry. Sometimes right after I bust they fall."

"No apologies, but if you can put them up, that will be good too."

He did.

It was obvious she wanted very little reminder of what life had made of him.

Opening up his small refrigerator he grabbed a cup of blood.

Smelling her intoxicating odor while having sex could've put her in harm's way despite being his wife. Lest they forget he was a Vampire. And so, he kept a small fridge stocked, to prevent going too far during the heat of passion where he would suck her dry.

"What are your plans for tonight?" Lying on her side, she whipped her hair over her shoulder. It brushed against her right and left nipple.

Sighing, he looked back at her and focused on the window. "How about you ask what you really want to know and stop wasting time."

"Can we have dinner tonight? Please. Just us two."

He drank every drop and laid on the bed face up. "We had dinner last night. And the night before that. And the night before—."

"Cage, I can't enjoy you during the day." She interrupted, rubbing her fingers through the lines of his muscles. "And since you only have the night to do what needs to be done, you often forget about me. So, I'm forced to take the time I have left."

"I get that, Angelina. But my life is different now."

"You heard me, Cage." She lowered her brow. "Will you have dinner with me or not?"

He didn't want to argue.

He wanted them to work and so, for tonight anyway, he decided to relent. "Yes, Angelina."

She won again.

"Thank you, thank you, thank you!" She yelled, hugging his back, which caused him to squeeze out a smile.

To get ready for a night on the town, Cage and Angelina took a shower face to face. Every time he stared into her eyes and inhaled the fruity odor of her skin he was reminded of the past. Of the times where things were not as complicated.

Now he knew too much.

Was expected to do too much.

While also juggling a new jealous wife.

After getting out the shower she dried him off and he did the same for her, before kissing her gently on the lips.

It was time to get a bit serious.

"Angelina, have you seen Onion?"

Her heart rate increased. "We never talk about him. Why...why you bringing him up now?"

"I'm waiting for an answer."

30   By T. Styles

"I'm afraid of him. Wouldn't be alone with him if he begged me to. So why are you asking me? Have I done something to make you distrust me?"

"No."

"Cage, when we got married you promised you'd leave him alone. But I hear whispers of his name when you think I'm not listening in this house. Did something change? Are you two fighting again?"

"I love you," he said firmly. "You never have to worry with me. All I see is you. All I want is your happiness."

"Cage, are you fighting with Onion again?" She bit at her lip which caused the blood to rush to the surface.

He wanted to suck it clear.

"No."

She didn't believe him.

And he didn't give a fuck.

Appeased for the moment, she hugged him tightly, their bodies pressed against one another.

Once they were done, they dressed in velvet red robes and walked toward their bedroom.

Within seconds, twenty-year-old Bloom and twenty-two-year-old Tatum walked up to him, on the way to their rooms. Both of them had grown tall and fit in stature, stereotypical of all Wolves.

But it was Bloom who pulled Cage tightly into an embrace. With her nose in the pit of his chest, she inhaled so deeply, it felt erotic.

Concerned, Cage peeled her off his body. "What you getting into tonight?" He asked them both.

"I'm about to go live on social media and Bloom is gonna sit in the background getting on my nerves again," Tatum said.

"Well, make time for me tomorrow," Cage responded. "I have some things I want to talk to you both about."

"Sure thing," Tatum nodded.

Bloom hugged Angelina and they both walked away.

Eager to leave and begin their night, Cage and Angelina continued to their bedroom only to be met by another visitor.

It was Arabia standing in front of the door. Curvaceous to the gods, her long curly hair ran down her back and she readjusted her red rimmed glasses as she stood, prepared to greet them.

But Angelina was not a fan of the woman.

Besides, Arabia was powerful and mysterious, and always wore a smile like a comfortable pair of shoes. Only taking it off when needing to get her point across.

More than anything, she had Cage's ear.

Which left the new wife without an identity.

"Angelina." She nodded at her to avoid being rude and focused on Cage again. "We have to talk."

"Actually, we were just getting ready to go to dinner." Angelina interjected, stepping forward. "I'm sure whatever you have to tell him can wait until the next day."

"It can't. He's a Vampire, remember? But I'll do my best to make things quick *tonight* so you can have whatever time that's left."

"Is everything okay?" Cage asked Arabia.

"I've been trying to catch up with you for the last few days. We must speak now."

Cage took a deep breath and turned around and faced his wife. "This won't be all night, but I have to see what it is she wants."

By T. Styles

"When will you ever put me first?" She threw her hands up in the air.

"What's that supposed to mean?"

"I always come last with you, Cage." She tossed a hand in Arabia's direction as if Arabia were a roach on the wall. "This is the perfect example. And the shit hurts because I would've never gotten--."

"What?" He asked, stepping closer. "You would've never gotten what, Angelina?"

She looked down.

"Married?" He said seriously.

"I wasn't going to say that."

He stepped even closer and rubbed her shoulders. "Listen, I know you were looking forward to tonight. And I really am sorry. But this is important. The Collective needs me."

"I need you."

"I know. So let me work to be quick." He kissed her on the cheek and walked away with Arabia, leaving Angelina alone.

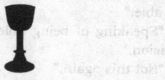

Cage stood with Arabia inside his massive living room. His robe was slightly open showcasing his chiseled physique. He would have gotten dressed first except she mentioned that speaking to him was urgent.

And so, she was on the receiving end of his delicious body.

Of course, she noticed.

The man was porn candy.

"This better be good," he sat in his recliner and waved for her to take a seat.

She remained standing.

"Sit." It was a demand. Not a request.

She obeyed.

"What do you need that can't wait until later? Because once again you have upset my wife."

She rolled her eyes. "You have to watch the clubs, Cage."

He shook his head. "This micromanaging shit is getting on my fucking nerves."

"I'm serious. You are royalty. Which means whenever you move you wear a crown that some people want to knock off. So running around in clubs is bad news."

"Listen, I'm doing what you wanted. I'm bonding with younger members of The Collective so that when its time, to do whatever the fuck you want me to do, I'm able."

"Speaking of being able, I need you to make a decision."

"Not this again."

"You have to understand how important choosing your collection is, Cage. Not only to you but to the Vampire Collective as a whole. You are Tino's son. That means your collection will be the model by which all collections are made and operated. We can't break tradition now."

"Why is it so important?" He got up and walked to his small refrigerator and grabbed a cup of blood. "I don't get it. Because the last thing I need is a bunch

34

of bitches hanging around me with Angelina feeling the way that she does right now." He pointed her way.

"She's an addict. An addict needs something to crave. For now, it's you."

She noticed the way his veins pulsated. And his brows lowered.

"Watch what you say about my wife!"

Arabia could feel his hate for her from across the room. "Have you noticed any other changes? In yourself?"

"What are you asking?"

"There will come a time, after you've been a Vampire for a while, where you will experience bouts of rage. I'm speaking about extreme rage. Some of these bouts lead weaker Vamps into some very dark places, while others control themselves. It's called Vampire Rage."

"What the fuck that got to do with my wife?"

"You're angry now. And to be honest, I'm scared. Because if you don't pay attention to it, you will hurt the people around you. You will ruin relationships with your allies. And you will hurt yourself."

"I would never do anything to hurt my niggas I fuck with. Which is why I want you to be careful with Angelina."

"You of all people know I'm not in the business of disrespecting Angelina or you. I'm at your side because we need you. *I* need you. And still, you'll have to decide at some point which is more important. Do you want to maintain a normal life, or do you want to lead? It can't be both. But understand that no matter what you choose, you are a Vampire."

Cage didn't feel like going over and over about getting a collection. He made up his mind a long time ago that he wouldn't. Believing there were other things more important.

Not only that...he didn't trust anybody except Shane and Ellis, his friends, who had the Vamp gene but had not taken The Fluid. Unfortunately, after helping him, both of them went missing and had yet to be found.

Since the person responsible he once considered a friend, it had him not trusting people. This was the main reason he didn't want to have a bunch of strangers around him.

Especially if it was true that at some point, he would be called to lead the Vampires to the slaughter, to protect Norms.

"What makes the collection so important?" He drank most of the blood in his cup.

"As you know already, when you are of The Fluid those who are connected to you feel what you feel. If something were to happen to you they would be injured greatly. As a result, they have a vested interest in keeping you alive. So, the collection is not just about numbers or even the Vampire Collective as a whole. It's about your personal safety."

He never thought about it that way.

In his mind he didn't want anyone around causing more problems with his connection to his wife and his siblings which was rocky at best. But now that Arabia raised a good point, maybe he should reconsider after all.

"Give me some time to mull shit over."

"I'll honor that. What about meeting with the Elders?"

He rolled his eyes. "You mean more people like you? Telling me what to do? Nah, I'm good."

"Cage. I'm serious. They want to meet you."

"What makes them so important?"

"They have been around for centuries. And can guide your efforts and--"

"Nah." He decided to answer her question with an equally important question. "Do you know where Onion is?"

"I made it clear that I don't want any parts of your past."

"But I need to find him to protect my future. So, I ask again, do you know where he is, Arabia? It's a simple question."

"Cage, think about what I said about your collection. Everything else doesn't interest me."

"Sometimes when I speak to you it's hard to remember who's in charge."

"I didn't know you had a problem with women leading. I learn something new every day."

"Don't mock me, Arabia. At some point if we're going to get along, you must give me the things I ask for. Or I will be forced to take them."

CHAPTER TWO
"What...what are you?"

He wasn't a star gazing type of nigga, but he did glance up for a moment and take in the beauty. The moon appeared to taunt him, while wondering why he would subject himself to such pain.

Still, he was looking for the beauty of another kind.

Anxious as usual, Onion sat on the curb outside of an abandoned restaurant. It shut down years earlier after a fire he set ravaged the property. Sponsored by Vamp Rage, he decided to act violently after waiting for his love, only for her not to show.

Embarrassed that the staff and customers thought he was a gump, he set gas to the spot and watched it light up the sky.

Now he could sit alone in his shame.

His car of the moment, a black Volvo with tinted windows was running. When the clock struck 9:00pm, he took a deep breath.

Nothing.

Disappointment washed over him when it was made clear that once again, she wouldn't show up.

He dragged two hands down his face and wondered why he bothered at all. Every night he had to build himself up to come to the location, hoping that for once things would be different.

Instead, they remained the same.

Years ago, before Angelina married Cage, she promised that whenever she thought he needed her, that she would show up to the first place they ate lunch as teenagers.

By T. Styles

This meeting would mean no strings would be attached and that the purpose would be to listen.

With no judgement of each other's current circumstance.

But that didn't happen.

Because despite needing her every hour, of every fucking night, she didn't show her face.

And that longing, coupled with Cage having what he felt belonged to him, had him eager to destroy worlds. Even if it be his own.

Standing up, he brushed the dirt off the back of his pants and walked toward his car.

Tomorrow night, he would return again.

And face the same pain all over.

Onion and three of his friends stood on the sidelines of a pool party hosted by a rich drug dealer in West Virginia. He was with Chatterbox, a fellow Vamp who he always called when he wanted to get into trouble and Spikes, the owner of a chain of strip clubs so raunchy, customers would have to change their clothes before returning home, due to the smell of rank pussy in the air.

Dressed in black jeans with a black shirt and a white gold chain with smoked colored shades, Onion was giving sex appeal and mystery.

But he was actually looking for his prey.

"So, what we waiting on?" Chatterbox asked as they looked at women standing around the pool.

"I wanna make sure the timing is right."

"You never told me how long we're going to do this." Chatterbox said. "Don't get me wrong, I'm with it. But if The Collective found out we were draining blood from the source, they would have us killed."

Onion was livid.

Especially since in his heart, he knew that they were priming Cage as they spoke to take charge.

"The only Vamp you need to be worried about is me." Onion said. "And we'll wreak havoc in these streets for as long as I fucking want. Until I destroy his world."

"You know what I love about you?" Spikes said.

"Nah but I know you gonna tell me anyway."

"You blood rich. And yet you still prefer to drink the natural way."

They all gave each other dap as they made their moves deeper into the party.

After seducing women to the point of having no choice but to follow them anywhere, Onion lured a beautiful girl with a big butt and a loudmouth into the bathroom.

The moment he closed the door, she immediately began attacking him by tearing into his clothing. He knew he threw on the charm but had no idea it was so good.

Shawty couldn't wait.

Bending her over, the palm of her hands touched the soiled toilet seat. Every time he had sex, it didn't matter when, he would close his eyes and imagine he was entering Angelina again.

And since he fucked on a regular, he had the same fantasy over a hundred times in the past six months.

The mark for the evening was nasty, but that wasn't the point of the night.

Nah, not this time.

After exploding his nut deep into her body, he turned her around. With his fangs low, he widened his smile so she could see his teeth.

It made him pleased to know that in other rooms throughout the house, Chatterbox and Spikes were doing the same.

"What the fuck is that?" She yelled. "What...what are you?"

"Who I am is a better question."

"Who...who are you?"

"My name is Cage Stryker. And if you live, after I've had my fill, I want you to tell everyone."

CHAPTER THREE
"That shit smells good."

Flow laid face up on his bed and he was placing bets. When he lost more money than he had, he turned to porn instead.

He had yet to satisfy his natural craving for the female persuasion. And as a result, he took to self-satisfaction which didn't hold the same weight.

One hand on his phone, the other on his 18-inch dick, he did his best to stroke the full length.

It wasn't working.

Besides, he was lying on the double bed inside of his uncle Row's house and his body stretched so far downward, that his feet hung off the mattress making the entire shit uncomfortable.

"Fuck it," he said tossing the phone down, tucking his meat into his boxers and sitting up on the edge of the bed. Scratching his muscular chest, he looked at himself in the full-length mirror across the way.

The man exuded sex and rage in a way that made him a hit for women. But he wasn't interested in a relationship. Because most females he considered boring.

There were other more pressing things on his mind.

Although years had gone by, he still despised his brother and felt like he was responsible for his father's death. And the fact that he had yet to tell him why he was murdered, made him intent on loathing him all the days of his life.

By T. Styles

And then there was the paper that was rightfully his that he hadn't been blessed with yet.

So why hadn't Cage, who was the executor of Magnus' estate, come up off his coins? Things settled a few weeks earlier after a lot of legal issues that Cage took control of per his mother's wishes.

This sponsored the new hate he was brewing for him.

Getting out of bed, his heavy footsteps walked across the way and focused on his features more closely.

All Wolf, he was mesmerized as the structure of his body continued to adjust for the better.

Muscles popped.

Dick print etched into his boxer briefs even on a soft.

And his hair was recently locked which was something that Wolves did in general although no one really understood why. Some said it was mental for the pack while others said it was in their DNA.

Regardless, the locs signified for Wolves, natural unity.

Well, that was the plan anyway.

After taking a shower and slipping into a pair of grey sweatpants, he slid to the kitchen and grabbed two frozen burgers. As he busied himself, Row's girlfriend gazed in his direction and quickly looked away, due to being in awe of Flow's sex appeal.

"You want one?" He asked, just to fuck with her head.

"N...no. I'm good."

He snickered, grabbed a frying pan, and seared them just enough to say he put the meat to pan. Meanwhile the center was as pink as a wet vagina.

No bread.

No condiments.

Once it was brown enough, he grabbed the meat from the pan and ate it whole. Juice ran down the sides of his mouth and dripped on his chest.

He let it remain.

When he saw Row's girl still looking his way, he winked and readjusted his dick to the other side.

Horny as fuck, she got up and walked away.

He laughed.

It wasn't like she could do anything with him if she wanted. A male Wolf's dick was large to ensure the female got pregnant. But once a female took a male Wolf, her pussy curved to the male Wolf's penis.

Forever.

That meant no other Wolf would want her in the same way. This often-made women territorial and violent if their men strayed too far.

For women, sex was a painful process too, as the female vagina was extremely tight with a hole the size of a pinky finger.

So, when a female chose a Wolf, she chose seriously, as the tissue would have to be torn to fit, thereby connecting them sexually for life.

It didn't mean that broken female Wolves couldn't have sex with another male after choosing. But it did mean that if she did, she would be isolated and banned from the pack for the rest of her life.

"Hey, nephew." Row said, walking to the kitchen. Wearing grey sweatpants and no T-shirt it was obvious that although Flow was all man he wasn't as mature physically as his uncle. This nigga was a vision to behold in body, height and yes, dick size. "What is that baby oil?" He wiped the grease off Flow's chest with his thumb.

44   By T. Styles

Flow readjusted and cleared his throat. "What up?" Suddenly he remembered he wanted to ask him a question that he never got around to. "I hear Vampires can smell blood, and even have strength. What--."

"Developed Vampires have way more powers than that."

Flow frowned. "Like what?"

"No one really knows." He sighed. "Is that what you wanted to know?"

"Wolves, what can we do?"

He scratched his chest. "Wow, we never told you?"

Flow shook his head no.

"In the beginning when you're angry or fearful, your body will respond. Your muscles will swell and—."

"Like a Wolf?"

"We don't turn into animals. But we maintain a lot of the traits. Like I was saying your muscles will swell slightly. If you need to claw, your fingernails will grow and the strength you possess will be that of fifty plus men."

"So, we could overpower a Vampire?"

"Why you asking?"

Silence.

"You ready for that meeting in a few days right?" Row moved toward the refrigerator.

Flow wiped his mouth with the back of his hand. "That depends."

Row stepped closer to exert his power.

It was Wolf shit.

"On what?" Row grabbed the black hair band off his arm and tamed his locs.

"On if you talked to Cage yet." Flow burped. "Because I'm sick of him not giving me my paper."

Row shook his head, grabbed a burger from the freezer and moved toward the microwave where he pressed start. "Listen, your brother has your--."

"Best interest at heart." Flow said sarcastically. "I'm tired of hearing that shit."

"You sound like you don't believe it's true." Grabbing his burger, he ate it while it was mostly raw and a bit frozen.

"I don't trust him. He killed my father and--."

"So, you're the judge and executioner now?"

"Nah! But what I want to know is why you, uncle Canelo and Uncle Shannon seemed to forgive so easily? He was your brother."

"And Cage is your brother, Flow. And I know you not trying to see it that way but it's true."

"What is it about him? Why is everybody protecting him like he's some fucking messiah?"

"Fall back. Learn your place. And you'll be okay."

Flow shook his head, walked over to the wall, and grabbed his car keys.

"Where you going? We have the bonfire tonight. In preparation for you, Bloom and Tatum to officially meet the pack."

"The only pack I give a fuck about is the bands Cage owe me. The rest of y'all niggas can suck my dick."

By T. Styles

Driving down the road in his black Mustang, on his way to the local butcher, Flow thought about what his uncle said about his brother. He could talk until he was white in the face, but it wouldn't change his mind.

He hated Cage with a passion and felt well within his rights to do so.

Literally, he wished he would be dead.

He wanted him dealt with and so he would make it his business no matter what to see it happen.

And to think he looked up to him at one point.

Trusted him with his whole life.

Now all of it was a waste of time.

After pulling up to the butcher he parked his car and triggered the alarm. Bopping inside he noticed immediately how his sense of smell heightened.

Literally as he stood in front of the counter, he could smell fresh meat coming from beef, pork, and other cuts.

But there was another aroma that was arousing him in a different way.

"Aye, Spag, what you got in here that's new?" He asked the butcher while eyeing the glass case. "That shit smells good."

"I don't know what you talking about. Everything in here is the same."

But it wasn't though.

So, what was the new odor?

As he looked at cuts behind the refrigerated glass, he couldn't pinpoint the luscious scent.

It didn't matter.

After placing his order, he stood up against the wall and looked at those who glanced his way. Every woman was either not his style or appeared too weak. The hunt for the right bitch had begun but he was coming up short.

What meat is that? He thought again to himself, inhaling the air deeply.

"Flow." He heard someone say with a deep voice behind him.

When he turned around, he saw Onion staring his way. He immediately stood on guard. Because if this nigga wanted the heat, it was whatever.

"What you want with me?" He took one step back.

Onion was dressed in all black, with Chatterbox standing a few feet to the back of him in protection mode. "You been knowing me since we were kids. And you ain't got no conversation for me all of a sudden?" He adjusted his shades.

"I'm not playing games with you. You called my name. Fuck is up?"

Chatterbox laughed at the young pup.

And Flow took notice at the rage in his eyes.

"I have some opportunities that just plopped into my lap." Onion said rubbing his hands together. "And I want to put you onto one."

"Why would you do that?"

"I've been seeing you around. Your uncle's treat you like a kid, but I know that there's more in you. Am I right?"

Flow inhaled deeper and the smell that tantalized him was heavier.

"I would appreciate it if you got to the point."

Onion rubbed his hands together. "Like I said, a money-making opportunity has fallen into my lap. In the night I move it with no problem but in the daytime the opps aren't as good."

"The struggles of a bloodsucker huh?" He said sarcastically. "I'm still trying to figure out what the fuck that has to do with me."

"Let's do this because you seem agitated and shit and it's turning me the fuck off." He reached into his pocket and handed him a solid black card with nothing but a telephone number raised in red. "When you want to line your pockets, give me a call. If not, stay broke and die."

CHAPTER FOUR
"I wouldn't think of playing those games."

Money was in the room where business was being conducted. And Cage knew they all thought he was outside of his league.

But he didn't give a fuck.

He was brokering a deal that in his opinion, would be the most important deal of his lifetime. And he would see to it that every man in the room knew that they weren't doing him any favors.

This was his paper.

He was king.

Sitting on the side of a long cherry wood mahogany table, with his lawyers to the right and left of him, he signed the final lines.

With a few strokes of his pen, the deal was done, and every member of E&I Services sighed collectively.

Cage slid the signature covered documents to his attorney instead of across the table where they were waiting.

"I trust everything is to your liking?" Warren from E&I Services asked with raised brows.

Cage looked up at him and shook his head. He hated stupid questions. "If it wasn't to my liking, I wouldn't be signing."

Warren cleared his throat. "It's just that we've done all we can to accommodate you and I thought everything would be finalized tonight. So--."

"Mr. Stryker would prefer it if you got to the point." Cage's attorney interjected. "We would too."

"It's just that we don't understand why you didn't give us the signed documents. After all, although

By T. Styles

we've accommodated you by meeting at night, we really would love to get home to our families."

"I just bought your company for millions." Cage chuckled once. "And you worrying about your pillow getting cold?"

"It's not that. It's--."

"My attorney is gonna verify everything else is in order." He rose, dusted the invisible fibers off his button-down black shirt and slacks. The *Magnus* white gold and diamond pendant chain glistened against the top of his tatted chest and neck. "I'm out."

Walking out the door without a word more, he slipped into his chauffeured Escalade.

"Where to boss?"

"The bank."

The moment he got situated in the backseat, his phone rang. Reluctantly he answered. "Hello."

"Where were you last night?" Arabia asked.

"You're playing right?"

"Cage."

"After meeting with you, I took Angelina out. You forgot already? Now what's up? What do you want?"

"Nothing. I just wanted to be sure."

He dragged a hand down his face. "Listen, I'm not with the games. Now either tell me what's going on, or the trust we built is going to falter."

"Someone said you were at the club and that you had bitten someone out in the open."

He frowned. "Fuck no that wasn't me."

"I knew it."

Cage shook his head and said, "If that's it I gotta bounce."

When the call was over, he thought about what she said. Could it be possible that Onion was trying to get his reputation cut up in the streets? Even though it could oust everyone, including The Collective.

When his phone rang again, he saw it was his wife. "What's up?"

"Where are you?"

Cage raked his hand through his soft, thick short cropped curly hair. "I have to make another stop and then I'll be home."

"Cage."

He glared. "Fuck is up with all these questions? Huh? I told you I would be in meetings all week. Just let me handle things so we can--."

"Do you know what today is?"

Of course, he didn't.

"Today was the day we first met."

Angelina kept track of anniversaries like a broker did bank balances. While other than the day they got married, Cage didn't give a fuck what day it was.

"We'll do something when we--."

"Cage. I'm lonely."

He took a deep breath. Breaking his wife's heart wasn't on brand for him. He loved Angelina.

Nah.

Scratch that.

He idolized her.

But it wasn't like he didn't already do his best to show her how much he cared. Spending fifty percent of his waking hours with her, which meant he had about six hours left, kept him strapped for time.

And still, to hear her yell it, it wasn't enough.

"You're going to have to find a hobby, Angelina. I want to be with you, but I don't want you consumed with me."

"Consumed?"

By T. Styles

He sat deeper into the seat. "Yeah. Like now, I said I have something to do. And you calling me about an anniversary that to be honest, I'm not recognizing."

Suddenly he remembered what Arabia said about his rep. Because if it was true that Onion was trying to put bodies on to his name, he didn't want it coming back to her, and destroying their already fragile bond.

"Before I go, do you remember me asking you about Onion the other night?"

"Of course, I do."

"Well, there's a reason. I want to talk to you about something that you must keep between us."

"You're scaring me."

"Will you keep it between us or not? Don't tell Bloom, Tatum or Flow."

"Of course. What's wrong?"

"Onion killed my father."

"That's...that's a lie."

He glared. "I put you on to truth and you call me a liar?"

"But...but it doesn't make any sense. You killed your father. You told both of us, remember?"

It was useless and obvious that she was set on believing what she wanted to believe. "Do you know where he is?"

"Cage, we have to talk. I don't like where this is go--."

He hung up in her face. He would blame it on a dropped call later. But for now, there were other things more important.

When the car stopped in the office park where a bank was located, he walked around back with his bodyguard at his side. Within seconds a door was opened and a man wearing a stiff designer suit appeared.

"Sir," he bowed his head to Cage.

"Thanks for meeting me tonight. I know it's after hours."

"Not a problem, Mr. Stryker. We have all of the papers drawn up per your request."

Once inside, Cage sat down and looked at the black leather bill folders that were etched in gold with each of his siblings' names impressed upon them.

Sitting at the table in front of him the Banker said, "As you can see, all of their accounts have been funded with the money from your father's estate. But are we accurate that you wanted your percentage of your father's estate divided amongst them also?"

"Yes." Cage didn't want a cent from his father's death and as a result, he arranged to divvy the cash amongst them instead.

"Just wanted to make sure. Because God forbid something happens to you. This is clearly the right thing to do."

"Whether it is or not is my business. Just stick to the details and do your fucking job."

The Banker cleared his throat. "The money will be dispersed to them per the monthly deposits you have outlined, and the remaining funds will be given to them fully at age thirty."

Cage looked over the paperwork and double checked it twice.

Everything appeared to be in order.

"Any questions?" The banker asked.

"No. Just a comment."

"I'm listening."

By T. Styles

"If you fuck my family over, I will destroy you and take every last dollar out this bitch."

He sighed and nodded once. "I wouldn't think of playing those games."

Cage was on his way home when Flow called. "I know it's late. But can you make time for me, big bro?"

Last night he was a regular ass Vampire and now everybody was hitting his phone up as if he were the hottest thing in town.

"I haven't heard from you in months and now you wanna talk? Seems off."

"Why the suspicion? We related right?"

He was his kid brother.

He had no choice.

And so, Cage had his driver pull up on the side of a laundromat per Flow's request. Once parked, he saw Flow's ride ahead.

Cage's driver/bodyguard opened the back side door and Flow slid inside.

The moon was high and bright.

Most of all, it was full.

"Brother." Cage said, while eyeing him cautiously. "What you need from me?"

Flow focused on the moon's magnificence and took a deep breath. "You remember when we were growing up and ma and dad would go to it at night? I mean they fought so bad, it felt like they would tear the roof off."

"Flow, I remember everything about them days. Even memories at an age I shouldn't know much about."

"I'm just understanding that when dad was his angriest, and me, Tatum, Bloom and Archer would get mad too, it was because of the full moon." He looked at Cage. "Most of all, I learned that we can be killed during a night like tonight. But I'm not concerned. Everybody got weaknesses, don't they?"

Cage nodded. "True. Every nigga that breathes dies."

"I hate secrets." Flow said looking into his eyes.

Cage sat back. "What's this shit about, little nigga? Speak your mind."

"Where's my money?"

"Do you need anything? Because I see to it that you get over three thousand a month. You eighteen-years old. You don't even have your own crib. So, what you need more paper for?"

"That's not the point."

"Bloom and Tatum not complaining. It's just you. If you not careful, the money gonna run out before--."

"But it's my money. If I spent every dime, that's my fucking problem."

That was true.

But Cage honestly thought at some point he wouldn't be around based on what Arabia told him. And so he wanted to make sure his siblings were financially set for life.

"And I asked you a question." Cage said. "What you need the money for?"

Flow smiled and looked at the moon again. Suddenly he took a long inhale. "Now that I'm older, I smell you better."

Chills.

Unlike most Vampires, Cage knew at some point, Wolves would crave Vamp flesh. Arabia made it clear that she and the Elders were keeping this a secret to prevent a premature war between the two breeds. So, his comment made him more than uncomfortable.

Would he make moves to kill his brother tonight?

"I'll get up with you later, Flow."

"You scared big brother?" His eyes twinkled.

"I won't tell you a--."

Suddenly Flow charged in his direction.

The thing was, Cage wasn't a Norm. So, he could definitely deal with the issue at hand.

Using his extreme strength, Cage shoved him so hard the door broke, and he fell out. Within seconds Cage's driver laid hands on him before Flow could rush his way again.

Picking him up off of his feet, he dominated control as Flow moved viciously to be released.

And then he stopped.

He just stared at Cage as if his light had been switched off.

"You scared?" Flow smiled. "All I wanted was a hug."

"Take him away before I go off." Cage said.

"Sure thing, boss."

As he was dragged off, he could hear him laughing.

Two things struck Cage at that moment.

First, he knew that if Flow desired, he could fling his bodyguard to the ground, and it wouldn't be a thing that could be done about it. Just like Vamps, Wolves were unusually strong.

So, the fight would be down to the most fed.

Or the angriest.

Second, Cage was certain that at some point, he and his kid brother were going to come to blows.

It was just a matter of when.

By T. Styles

CHAPTER FIVE
"Where they are is very dangerous."

When Cage woke up, a little after 7:00pm, he was surprised to see Angelina still asleep next to him. For some reason her being sleep gave him a sense of relief. Lately he didn't feel like the emotional weight she pressed upon him daily.

She could sleep all day for all he gave a fuck.

Just as long as when he wanted the pussy, it would be in his bed, soft, warm and ready.

Easing out of bed, and jumping in the shower, he walked to his dining room where he knew Arabia was waiting for their nightly brief.

When he opened the door, she was sitting at the end of the table with a yellow legal pad in front of her. Since this was planned, he sat on the far opposite end and braced himself.

"Is she still asleep?" She asked.

He nodded. "For now."

"You can move closer, you know. I don't bite." She responded.

He laughed once. "You may not bite yet. As of now, there's still space in my Fluid Line." He joked.

She laughed lightly.

He smiled.

"Nah, I need access in the daytime to be able to help you."

He heard from Gordon, his teacher who died trying to save his siblings years ago, that she was angry in the morning due to having the gene. Since he only saw her at night, he wondered if this was true.

"What do you have for me? We have to be quick before Angelina wakes."

She nodded and looked at her list. "I have fifty."

"You mean forty-nine."

"I'm not talking about the fifty needed to convert members of your collection. I'm talking about fifty *new* members of your collection."

"Wait, you want me to bring fifty members into The Collective? Why?"

"You'll need to solicit respect from other collections. Having numbers that deep will help."

He got up and walked to the refrigerator to grab a cup of blood. "How long have you been scouting for me?"

"Since the day you were born."

He took a sip and squeezed his lips clean. "I don't get it. Why that many? And why that much planning?"

"Your father and Gordon both knew what I also know to be true. That you, being raised by Magnus, meant you were the answer to the future. Your bravery will save a lot of people. And so, we needed to make sure that those invited to be in your collection are worthy."

"Wow. This the long con."

"We are aware of their backgrounds. Their parents. What they believe and their morals. And each one of them, every single one, have been waiting for this moment. More importantly, if you ask, they will die for you."

This was the first time he realized how deep the king thing really was. "You mentioned that at some point, to save Norms, I would have to lead my own people to the slaughter. What does that look like?"

"We never really know the time. What usually happens is that Wolves begin to crave the flesh of Vampires."

"But that's happening now."

"Yes, but it's sporadic. When it is time for the slaughter, Wolves will crave Vamp flesh so much that it can't be denied. During this occurrence, we'll have a meeting, preferably with the Elders, and you'll arrange to have Vampires, at least a thousand, go to a specified location. The Wolves will smell the scent due to how many will gather. On this land, *The Fringale*, there will be a battle. Some Wolves will die. All Vamps will die. And the balance will be reset."

Cage looked down.

"What is it, Cage?"

"I don't know...I don't know if I can turn on my own people. I mean when I look at some of these Norms, the ones who ooze this sweet odor, I'm reminded that they have already given up on life. Otherwise, we wouldn't crave their blood. So why should we care about them?"

"We care because the purpose of life is to get Norms to see their power."

"How can we do this if they don't know about us? If they knew that we hunted them due to their own actions, then maybe it would be worthwhile."

"Cage, don't try to change things. Just go with the flow. It's always been this way." She paused. "Can we talk about your fifty now?"

He decided to go a little off topic. "Before I review your list, I need to know where *they* are first."

She sighed. "Cage, I don't know what you're talking about. Plus, we can't keep wasting time. You must--."

"You know who I'm talking about." His eyes narrowed.

"This is pushing us further from the goal."

"They helped me. When I needed them the most. And after Savannah got into the mix, she did something to them. If they're dead, I'll deal with it. But I need them brought to me for their families. I need Shane and Ellis. And since you know everything, I need you to tell me where they are."

A little over a year ago, Savannah, who Cage thought was a friend, kidnapped his siblings. And when Shane and Ellis, who were once her allies, decided to help Cage instead, she abducted them too.

He believed they were alive.

And he believed Arabia knew where to find them.

"I respect you. But if I'm your king, you will give me an answer right now. Or all this shit we doing is done. That's not a threat. That's a promise."

She sighed and sat back. "I know where they are."

"I know you do." He leaned forward. "How long have you known their location?"

"From the start."

He shook his head. "I'm converting my members too. I want them in my fifty."

"But they aren't the right type. And how do you know they'll want to take The Fluid anyway? It can be a--."

"You just sat across from me at this table and said you picked my entire collection. And I never met none of them."

"But I have and--."

By T. Styles

"I don't know none of them niggas!" He yelled, banging his fist on the table. It fractured under his blow and his fangs dropped. "So, if you want me to accept these *forty-eight*. You'll give me the two. And let's be clear, this is not up for discussion or negotiation."

She readjusted. "Okay. I'll tell you but there's more."

"I'm listening."

"Where they are is very dangerous. It won't be easy to get them."

"Then I guess we gotta go in the Vampire way."

When the meeting was over, when he returned to his bedroom, Angelina was gone.

As usual, Onion sat on the curb in front of the abandoned restaurant waiting. It was two minutes before 9:00 o'clock, and his heart thumped when he saw Angelina pull up in a two-seater white BMW.

Was he seeing things?

Quickly he rose and smiled as he moved in the direction of the car.

Parking any kind of way, she flung the door open, leaving it ajar. As she stomped toward him, wearing a black one-piece catsuit and a white fall jacket, he took one step back and another forward.

She was breathtaking.

And the scent of lavender and peaches lit the air.

"Is it true?" She asked, hand on the hip.

Her hair blew in the wind and when he stared at her body, his fangs dropped. What he wouldn't give for a bite.

Just one little taste.

"I...I can't believe you showed up." He looked her over. Taking in every inch of her beautiful face for later. "I have missed—."

"Is it true? Did you kill Magnus?"

Damn. He thought. *That nigga told.*

"I came here every day for years, only for you to step to me about that dude. What I gotta do? Kill his ass so he won't be a fucking factor no more?"

"Don't threaten my husband!"

His nostrils flared. "Your husband! Do you realize what you gonna make me do to this man? I fucking love you and you step to me with this after I haven't seen or heard from you in years?"

This wasn't going as planned.

Anger drove her to meet him in their special spot. But she was so mad that she forgot about its original purpose. To be a safe space where they would always hear each other out.

Still, this was serious.

Taking a deep breath, she remembered that she was in the middle of two killers. It was important to tread lightly. "Did you kill Magnus?"

Onion walked away and stopped.

He had to play this carefully. If he lied and there was a way to validate the truth, he would lose her forever.

After a brief delay, he chose a plan, hoping that the love he believed she still had for him, would be enough to bring her back.

Returning he said, "Yes."

Her shoulders drooped. "W...why?" She placed a hand over her heart. "I saw the guilt Cage had about this shit. You were there with us. How could you let him hold that type of pain when it was your fault?"

"Because Tino was concerned that Magnus wasn't raising him right. So, he wanted Magnus dead. The plan was for Cage to get closer to The Collective. But things didn't pan out."

"And you had me believing it was him the entire time."

Onion moved to touch her hand, but she pulled away.

"Please, Angelina. I'm still the same nigga I was when we were kids. I'm still the same nigga who would protect you no matter what. If I could take that shit back, I would."

She wiped the hair out of her face, looked down and slowly met his gaze. "I don't believe you. And if I don't believe you, I can never trust you."

With that she ran to her car, drove off, leaving him enraged.

CHAPTER SIX
"You promised them they would be blood rich by now..."

In the bathroom of a club, Onion had a Norm planted against the wall as he fucked her methodically.

Originally the plan was to bring her to an abandoned house and take a few bags of blood from her flesh. But she smelled so sweet due to her desperate nature that he had to taste her now.

While he eased in and out of her pussy, he bit down into her neck and sucked slowly.

The worst part was that he hadn't given her a roofie and as a result she was wide awake witnessing something she was having a hard time understanding. And it was that a Vampire was biting into her flesh. At the same time his dick strokes felt so soothing that she found herself letting go despite her body growing weaker.

After he came inside of her pussy she dropped to the floor.

"Who are you?" She whispered.

"My name's Cage Stryker. If you live, tell everyone."

Before Onion's vendetta to ruin Cage's name, there were only whispers that Vampires were real. But he was proving to be more reckless by the day. He wanted the world to know what was going on right under their noses.

He wanted the world to know Cage Stryker's name.

By T. Styles

And he would drag The Collective and his fate into the picture too if he had to.

After he was done, he eased into his car and sped home. If things went to plan, he would ruin Cage's world before he laid eyes on him again.

This, he felt, would eventually bring Angelina back to his bed where she would remain until her dying days.

Once he got home, he wasn't surprised to see Cheddar sitting in his lounge waiting. His legs were crossed ankle to knee, and he was smoking a cigar. "So, this is your plan?"

"Let's talk about you entering my house without asking." He walked past him.

"You won't see me any other time. And I'm done playing games. Either we're working together or we not."

Onion looked at him once and returned his attention to his bar. Pouring himself a hefty glass of wine, he sat across from him. "I think you're getting confused on the chain of command up in this bitch. You don't question me. I question you."

"Your power only goes as far as the people who serve you. And now, outside of a few sewer Vamps, no one respects you."

"Are you threatening me?"

"I'm giving you facts. Power is best expressed by the people who will lay down their lives for you. And it looks like due to your obsession with Cage, nobody will do that will they?"

"You're still here."

"Am I?" He leaned forward.

"If you have something on your mind, say it and stop wasting my fucking time."

Cheddar placed his cigar in the ashtray. "Before you started this beef with Cage, when Tino was alive, you had about fifteen people who would ride with you. You promised them they would all be blood rich by now, never having to hunt if they didn't want to."

"And?"

"And you lied. So, guess what, with the exception of Chatterbox who talks too fucking much, and Spikes, the sewer Vamps left you too."

"That's not true. I still have the undergrounds. The people working the bars and the strip clubs in the whorehouses."

"Let me put it like this...everybody of importance bounced. The ones you think are still in your camp are lying to you because they're waiting in case you win the war with Cage. Meanwhile Cage has been mostly quiet and gaining the approval of The Collective, due directly to his relationship with Arabia and being Tino's blood. The way things look now, your days are numbered."

"I got some plans too."

"Running around clubs, fucking and biting bitches on the neck while giving them Cage's name ain't it."

Onion was so angry he knew about his weak ass plan that his jaw twitched.

"Yep, Chatterbox really does talk too much. You look surprised though. I'm not. That's why his own master banished him."

"You bring a lot of issues. But where are the solutions?"

"The way things are going right now, if there's a blood bounty on your head, you have people who have direct access to you who are willing to oblige.

There's no reason for them to protect you. They aren't vested in you remaining alive."

"I'm waiting for the solution."

"It's time for you to pick a collection."

He waved the air. As far as Onion was concerned, the conversation was over. "I don't feel like begging 49 old ass Vamps to help me convert."

"I have some people who will help convert but we need more. I also have people who want to be a part of your Fluid Line for different reasons. Vanity for some. Blood chasing for others. Being of your line they will protect you even if they don't respect you. You don't have an option, Onion. As of right now, respect is not something that you can solicit. But that can change with time."

Onion was annoyed.

"So, either you want to survive, or you don't. Maybe we should start there."

"Don't test me, Cheddar. I value your opinion. But that doesn't mean I won't have you killed for disrespect."

"We gone past testing at this point. We're stating facts. Don't nobody fuck with you. They don't even like you. And that means instead of protecting your body they'll try to get it that head instead."

Onion shifted a little.

The truth was hard and he was about to start swinging.

"You need to choose a collection," Cheddar continued. "And you need to do it now."

"Aight."

Where was the fight?

Cheddar was low-key shocked. Lately it seemed the only thing Onion was interested in was getting at

Cage's bitch and brother. He also made efforts to buy up all the Vitamin D he could find, to eventually poison him.

But they learned that Cage didn't drink gifts of blood from Vampires he didn't know.

So that plan was easier said than done.

"How do we go about getting the members? Because before I agree, I need to meet them first."

"I have a few people I'm looking at right now who will join your collection. But the total will be about twenty. Now finding all of the forty-nine to help you convert will be harder."

"I was Tino's right hand for years. And this is the thanks I get?"

"Like I said, nobody wants to be associated with you. But everything will work out. If we find forty-nine to help convert, go old school, and turn over fifty Vamps that night too who are looking to belong. So, you won't waste the evening on just one."

"Okay, so now we need more collection members so--."

"This won't be easy," Cheddar said, cutting him off.

"Why?"

Cheddar sighed. "They're hoping Cage will choose them first."

This made Onion all the angrier. For one, he had to deal with Cage stealing Angelina. And now he had to fight for the scraps of whatever was left to build his collection.

"Find me the converters. And fifty who want to be in my collection. But there are a few prerequisites."

"There always is."

"My patience with you is thinning."

"I'm listening."

70   By T. Styles

"They have to be grimy. Vamps who would do whatever is required of them. No matter what I ask."

"So, you want untrustworthy people around you?"

"Honesty is subjective. As long as I can trust them to be exactly who they are, for my plans that'll be enough."

CHAPTER SEVEN
"Go deeper."

Cage walked the mall with Bloom. The smell of fruit was intoxicating and yet he learned to control his urges instead of snatching a woman, yanking her behind the property and having his fill like the whispers were claiming.

But it was definitely easier said than done, the more powerful the odor.

Bloom, on the other hand, had gotten so beautiful over the years that every five minutes men would turn their heads to look at her, despite walking with Cage.

Even though she was definitely fine, she still took knife jabs to her skin on a regular basis, which bothered him greatly.

"So, I spoke to Tatum, and we decided not to get the apartment," she blurted. "We wanna stay with you instead."

He paused and looked over at her. "What changed your mind?"

She inhaled deeply and Cage backed up. Not that he was scared, but he was concerned that Wolves were picking up on their scents too soon.

"We decided we wanted to stay at your house. To help out and all."

"Bloom, don't get me wrong I'm glad you're staying but both of you made a big deal about getting your own places last month. I want to make sure you aren't doing it for me."

"You live in a mansion. You have servants and people to cook for us. Even if we leave and have a nice

72 **By T. Styles**

apartment nobody will take care of us like you do. Besides, we want to look after you while you sleep."

"I have a wife to do that."

She looked away.

What was that? He thought.

Cage stepped closer. "Bloom, talk to me."

"I want to stay out of it."

He grabbed her shoulders softly. "Tell me what's on your mind."

"Sometimes when I get up in the morning to get a burger or whatever I'll check on you. To be sure you're okay."

"Go deeper."

She tucked her hair behind her ear. "A few times I caught her..." She paused and that made him uncomfortable.

"Little sister, I need you to talk to me."

"I caught her having sex with you while you slept."

Releasing his hold, Cage was so consumed with embarrassment that he didn't know where to start. "First off, you shouldn't come into my room in the morning. You know I don't like you to see me in that state."

"I'm sorry, but I just want to make sure you're there."

"Go deeper."

"Before you bought this house and you found us, you were gone for so many years. And we were afraid you wouldn't come back and save us from Savannah. That's a fear I still have. It's a fear all of us have, that one day we'll be forced underground again."

"As long as I'm alive, that will never happen. And I know you're worried, but I did come back."

"Not in the same way though, Cage. And now even though we're together, we don't get a chance to see you. You're either with Angelina, Arabia or..." Suddenly she began to hyperventilate.

"Bloom, calm down." He said softly.

Her breathing rate continued to speed up.

"Bloom, I need you to breathe."

It seemed like forever but finally she was calmer.

"Listen, I'm not going anywhere. And no one will put you in a hole anymore. Okay?"

"I know...I know. It's just that, sometimes I get scared. So, I come to your room to be sure you're still there. To be sure it's not a dream. And I saw what I saw but I don't want you mad at me either."

"I get it." He wiped a few of her tears away and before he could take his hand back, she kissed it while exposing her teeth.

This action closely resembled a bite.

"Bloom, are you okay?"

"Brother, why do you smell so good?"

"It's a new cologne."

"Well, never get rid of the smell. Please. I love it too much."

He couldn't shake the feeling that just having his siblings around him, put his life in immediate danger. Because although Vamps couldn't be killed in the traditional sense, they could be eaten alive.

He nodded and backed away. "Listen, let me worry about what you just told me. Don't say anything to Tatum or Angelina. In the meantime, how are you? Do you need anything else?"

Silence.

"Bloom."

"I feel like I don't have a life. And like everything I do, is for no reason. I want passion. I want to belong."

74   By T. Styles

"Have you connected with the pack?"

"The women there aren't like me. They're all too busy trying to choose a male Wolf."

"Try harder. Eventually you'll find friends who move like you do. Give it some time."

They were beautiful.

Perfect even.

Arabia, Gordon, and his father did well when they selected the future members of Cage's Collection many years ago.

Dressed in all black with a hint of red per Arabia's request, there in Cage's lounge stood twenty-five women and twenty-five men. Most had the Vamp gene, while the others had to be bitten along with The Fluid ceremony in order to be converted.

Since most collections took on the last name of their leader, they would be known as The Stryker Collection. Although the last name was not necessary, a name was usually recommended all the same.

With brief intros, one by one Cage shook each of their hands.

When he was done, he stood in front of them proudly and he could tell they had been waiting on this moment all of their lives. Since he still didn't take his power seriously, he didn't get the admiration.

But he knew it was necessary.

"I don't know what our future holds," Cage started. "But I promise you this, I will respect you and never ask of you something I wouldn't do myself."

They nodded and grinned brighter.

But there was one, with smooth brown skin and hazel eyes who stood out from the rest. Her natural camel colored hair ran down her back and her body rocked the imaginations of every man who looked her way.

They called her Helena.

And she didn't take her eyes off of him for one second.

He noticed her too.

"In the meantime, a date for our fluid ceremony has been set. I'll meet with each of you individually before that time."

They all applauded.

While Langley, a 27-year-old boxer, raised his glass high. "Whatever you need it's done, boss."

"Yes, we're all looking forward to serving you," Helena cheered.

Their eyes remained locked until Cage said the meeting was over.

When everyone dispersed and celebrated being officially chosen by Cage, Langley walked over to him instead.

"Sir, can I talk to you in private for a moment?"

Cage saw the seriousness in his eyes and tapped his shoulder for him to follow his lead to the corner where they could get a hint of privacy. "What's up?"

"I wanted to show you something."

Cage nodded.

76

Langley removed his cell phone and keyed up a video of several women talking about the legend of Cage Stryker. Video after video depicted tales of women speaking about how he bit them on the necks after a mysterious sexual encounter.

But it was the comments that had him shook.

Many of the women wished that they could experience what the women had spoken of, and all of the bitten ones who were on the brink of death, were considered to be lucky.

"This wasn't me." Cage said.

"I know, sir. I mean, I haven't known you long, but I can't imagine you moving like this when the goal has always been for The Collective to remain unseen."

He looked behind him at Arabia who was speaking to the others. "Did you show--."

"No, sir. I didn't show anyone but you. Definitely not Arabia."

"Why not?"

Silence.

"Langley, why didn't you show her?"

"The truth is, I don't trust her."

He nodded.

Having liked him already.

"Before you lose daylight, and take The Fluid, look into this for me."

Langley gazed down and back at him.

"What is it now?" Cage asked seriously.

"I never wanted anything more than I wanted this but if you need me, to remain in the day, I won't take The Fluid, sir."

"Not necessary. Just see what you can find. If you hear anything about Onion, let me know. Because if this is his bullshit out here, I gotta kill this nigga before he destroys everything I'm trying to create."

Langley smiled. "And I'd love to help."

What they didn't know was that Angelina heard every word said.

By T. Styles

CHAPTER EIGHT
"What you're trying to do is control my moves."

Having just got out the shower, she was naked when Cage walked through the door; and he hated her for it.

"Put some fucking clothes on, Angelina."

"Nigga, what?" She jumped up from the bed and stormed in his direction. "I heard about you having sex in clubs, Cage!"

Damn.

"Stop playing with me," he snapped, not knowing what else to say.

"Stop playing? You've been in the clubs every other night. If it's not true, why are these women saying it?"

"Maybe you should ask your boyfriend." He tossed the robe in her face.

She slid it on and crossed her arms tightly over her body. "I know you are avoiding the question on purpose."

"I don't know what's going on in the streets. But everything that's happening now, with me taking a collection, is to make sure that I'm safe. So that I can make sure that you and my family are safe too. That's all I care about."

She took a deep breath. "Well, what about the chick? The one you plan to put into your collection."

He walked past her toward his closet. "I don't have time for this, Angelina."

"The woman with the hazel eyes and the hair to match. You saw her. I know you did."

He shook his head. "We talked about this in great detail already. They're a part of my future collection and--."

"I'm not talking about them. I'm talking about her. Just her." She slammed her fist into her palm.

He stormed in her direction. "No, what you're trying to do is control my moves. And I won't let it happen."

"It's like you don't even respect or love me anymore! You don't even...you don't even like the sight of my body anymore."

He walked toward his side of the bed. "You tend to make things about you. It's not going to work this time."

She shivered with rage. "If you don't want me, maybe someone else will."

He never heard her wage such a heavy threat towards him before. And to be real, in that moment, it made him look at her differently.

And not for the better.

"Is that why you walking around here like a slut? In the hopes that somebody will stab that tired ass box out. So, you can have an excuse to step out on this marriage?"

He was punching each of her insecurities with no let up. This was not her husband, she was certain. "Cage, I—."

"Nah, you like to wait until a nigga sleep so you can jump on the dick." He grabbed it and rocked it to the right. "That way you get to pretend you still in need when I wake up."

"What...what are you talking about?"

By T. Styles

"I'm talking about this...if you ever make a threat to me like that again there won't be any us. There won't be any of this." He pointed between them. "Fuck up out my face!" He stormed out.

He knew she wasn't coming, but Onion would rather sit on the curb in anger, than to miss the one night she showed up to find him not there.

To his surprise, Angelina arrived on time.

Standing up slowly, he walked toward her, and they stared at one another.

Looking down she said, "I don't know what I'm doing here."

Onion was so afraid to say the wrong thing that he remained silent instead.

Smart move.

"I...I know there's no way we can go back to the way things were," she whispered. "The three of us, like when we were kids. When the chore was only to keep one another safe. But I still...I still desire it in my heart." She placed a hand on her chest. "Onion, are you doing something to Cage? Do you, do you still hate him?"

"I don't hate the nigga," he lied. "I just feel a kind of way because...because..."

"He started the beef with you and Tino?"

"No, because he took you from me." He grabbed her hand softly.

This time she didn't pull away.

Progress was made.

"I shouldn't be here. I...I'm married."

"All I want to be is a friend. Nothing more. Nothing less. You gonna deny me that shit when you know nobody loves you more than I do? Not even your fucking husband."

She looked away from his handsome face.

As the years went by, Onion's dark chocolate ass had gotten sexier. There was something to the Vampire shit that hit right, this was certain.

"I gotta go." When she moved to leave, he pulled her hand slightly and placed the other hand on her waist.

"Let me show you something." He said, his warm breath cascading down on her. "I won't violate your relationship."

"My marriage." She corrected him quickly.

"I just want to show you something and then you can go back to him. Do you still trust me?"

Ten minutes later they were walking into the apartment that was once rented by her cousin. The last time Angelina was there, she had just gotten caught fucking Cage and Onion reacted violently because of it.

Fear overcame her when the memories returned.

"Why am I here?" She backed up toward the door.

"I own this building and put it in your name."

Her eyes widened. "W...why?"

"So that you would have something just for you. That was all yours."

"Onion, I...didn't ask for this."

"I know." Slowly he moved toward her. "I brought you here because the last time we were here, together, I threatened your life. I walked in on...on something that hurt me. That still hurts to this night. You and Cage, two people I loved more than anything in this world, having sex."

"Onion, what's this about?" She trembled.

"Listen, baby," he said softly. "I don't want you afraid of me. I just...I just want you to know that while my feelings were valid, scaring you was wrong. And I'm so sorry I did that shit. It's just that there is nobody in this fucking world that I want more than you. And I would never have killed or converted you. I love you too much for that shit."

Angelina immediately felt relieved.

"Do you forgive me, Angelina?"

The love he had for her was on full display. What she wouldn't give for Cage to look at her the same way.

"I forgive you. But I will never leave Cage. I hope you understand that, Onion."

He didn't.

In fact, hearing the words pushed him on the brink of insanity. He would deal with him for sure.

"I just want to be in your life. Fuck everything else. Can you let me do that?"

Onion stood with Chatterbox in another lounge.

Although the plan was to dethrone Cage by causing havoc in the background, he, and Chatter both enjoyed the act of taking blood naturally from the source.

They were looking for their next victim when they heard a group of women talking not too far away from where they stood.

"Girl, if I get pulled into the bathroom tonight, leave me alone," a chubby brown skin girl said as she adjusted her hair. "I want to get bit and I want the dick too."

They all laughed.

Onion looked at Chatterbox and back at the girls.

"So, you think that Vampire shit is true?" One of them asked.

"If it is or isn't, it's sexy all the same."

"Well, bitch, if it is real, how you know he'll pick you and not me?" One of the others asked as she nudged her playfully. "He may be..."

As the women continued to chatter, it became painfully obvious that instead of being scared, she was ready to meet the great Cage Stryker in the flesh.

So instead of destroying his brand, Onion was helping to grow his legend.

The women were ready.

Making them more enamored with Cage than ever before.

"They liking this shit," Chatterbox whispered to Onion. "This ain't on plan. What we gonna do?"

"Stay right here."

"You want me to stay on--"

"Stay right here, nigga!" He yelled. "What the fuck."

Chatterbox nodded as Onion stormed away.

84

Grabbing brown skin girl's hand, Onion pulled her toward the bathroom. But it didn't go as planned.

"Ugh, get the fuck off me!" She yelled. "I'm not with that crazy shit."

He looked at her, smelled her fruity odor and his fangs dropped. "Are you going to come with me?"

He needed permission.

Her stomach rumbled and she felt faint.

It was one thing to talk shit, and it was a whole different matter to actually see a Vamp.

Her eyes blinked rapidly. "Y... y..."

After seducing her with his presence he said, "I need you to say yes."

"Yes." Her response didn't feel within her control.

Five seconds later, he pulled her into the men's bathroom.

Entering a stall, he pushed her lightly against the wall. "Remove your clothing."

Piece by piece she took off everything that hid her skin. Walking up to her, he unleashed his dick and raised her up so that her legs were straddling his sides.

Fear covered her eyes.

"You scared?" He asked, his fangs still hanging low.

She nodded.

"I thought this was what you wanted."

She remained silent as he moved in and out of her pussy. Right before he came, he said, "I'm going to bite you now. And when I do, you're going to die. Okay?"

She nodded once more.

"But before I do that, I want you to do me a favor."

Caught in his trance, and yet fully aware, she nodded once more.

Biting her neck, he took a bit of her own blood and dripped it on her fingertip. "Write the name Cage Stryker on that wall."

Doing as he instructed, she inscribed every word clearly.

When the last letter was drawn, he drained her dry and left her for dead.

Rain pounded against the tinted windows of Cage's vehicle.

There was something heavy on his mind that was certain.

Even though he shared everything with Arabia he didn't tell her one thing in particular. And it was that he spent every waking moment wanting to get back at Onion.

If he were able to tell her his reasoning, perhaps she would understand. At the same time, he knew she was of the old way of thinking.

And so, he kept his secrets to himself.

But that didn't stop him from soliciting help within The Collective.

Once parked, he eased out of his ride and approached three rogue Vampires. They didn't belong to any collection, as their masters died many years ago.

By T. Styles

As a result, they took odd jobs for those in power within The Collective to make ends meet. He didn't trust them as far as he could see them. Luckily this meeting wasn't about loyalty. He needed the grimiest of the grimiest on the case, if he was going to find the holes Onion frequented.

Standing in front of them, he inhaled the air deeply.

They all frowned.

Cage stepped closer. "There's another Vampire here!" He yelled out. "Show yourself!"

"Cage, I don't know what you're talking about. It's just us so--."

"Don't make me tell you again!"

The three looked at one another strangely. Up until that point it was uncommon to detect the scent of your own kind.

So how could Cage do it so effortlessly?

Berg whistled hard, and suddenly the Vampire hiding behind the dumpster in the alley came into view.

"Don't play games with me again," Cage said seriously to Berg and the hider. "Now where's Onion?"

"We still haven't found him," Berg said, clearing his throat.

"So let me get this straight, basically you're wasting all my time by calling this meeting?"

"It's not that we're wasting your time. We're trying to get what you need without letting everyone know you're looking. Basically, we need better incentives."

"So, you need more blood."

"We aren't trying to be greedy." Berg continued. "But some Vamps are aware that you're looking for him. And since Tino died, many are still choosing sides."

"What does that have to do with me?" He shrugged.

"They're afraid that this fight between you and Onion will put the Norms onto our existence. So, by giving them more blood, they may be inclined to come around and get involved. To help you versus Onion."

"Betting against me is the wrong move."

"We know. They don't. But...there's a reason many feel this way." Berg reached into his pocket and showed him a video. "This happened last night."

Standing in the alley, Cage looked at a video of a crime scene at a nightclub. What caught him the most was that at the end, the name Age Stryke was used.

"*Age Stryke?*" He handed him back the phone. "What does that have to do with me?"

"This is Onion working overtime to destroy your rep. This nigga so foul he's willing to bring us all down in the process."

Cage was heated. "Go deeper."

"We heard on the streets that a Vamp named Chatterbox was with him the night this happened. And that Onion had sex with the girl in the bathroom and wrote your name. We believe that an elder learned about the incident and did their best to change the name up. Hence *Age Stryke* instead of Cage Stryker."

"Why not wipe it off?"

"They feared pictures had been taken already." Berg sighed. "And it was best to cause confusion than heighten suspicion."

Cage walked away for a moment.

"Sir, we have a plan. We just want permission to execute it."

He turned around. "What have you come up with?"

"Onion's vain. So, we will attack his ego."

Cage walked in his direction. "Your games are your games. At the end of the day, I want Onion brought to me. And unless that shit happens, anything else won't be good enough." He moved even closer. "And you can tell everyone that's going against me this...there will come a time where I will be in full power. And I will remember when they chose to deny me."

He walked away.

Irritated, Cage trudged through his front door when Langley approached. He was so angry about the drama Onion was causing on the streets that his fangs remained low.

"What information do you have for me?"

"Sir, your fangs," he said lightly.

He walked toward his lounge. "What is it?"

"I have the address of some key Vamps in Onion's camp. But due to his recent actions, more of them are leaving. So, I won't be surprised if he's about to make his own collection to stay protected."

Cage walked to the refrigerator and grabbed a cup of blood. Drinking it all he said, "I want you to get in contact with someone named Berg. I'll give you his info. Just make sure he's doing all he can to find the people still surrounding Onion. If I can't get at Onion directly, I'll have to weaken the people in his camp instead."

He ran his tongue over his fangs and finished his blood.

Later on, that night Cage decided to question the one person he hoped couldn't provide him answers. Because if she did know what he needed to know, it meant she was going against him and seeing Onion behind his back.

When he opened the bedroom door Angelina was in front of her vanity brushing her hair.

She was happy.

Fuck for?

"You're home early." She said softly, placing the brush down.

He walked in and closed the door. "Yeah, I'm here."

"I wanna say I'm sorry about our argument over your collection, Cage. I still don't understand a lot about everything but I'm trying desperately. And I hope you know that."

By T. Styles

He walked up to her, and she rose. Standing in front of her he said. "I forgive you."

"Then why do you look like something's on your heart?"

"Do you ever feel like you made a mistake? And that you should've chosen him instead?"

She felt slightly dizzy. "I'm confused, Cage." She giggled due to being nervous. "Now tell me what's on your mind."

"Listen, if you tell me the truth right now, I won't be mad. But if it comes out later that you know, and you hid the truth behind my back, I will hurt you." He squeezed her arms lightly. "Now do you know where Onion is?"

She walked away.

Far back.

Did he know? She thought.

"Cage, Onion's a Vamp too. Even if I wanted to, I couldn't see him in the daytime. And at night unless you have plans, we're always together."

"Not always. You've been absent a lot lately."

"Cage, stop it!"

He moved quickly toward her, defying the laws of gravity. "Why aren't you answering my question?"

Her heart thumped. How did he move so fast?

She looked down and slowly up into his eyes. "I promise you; I don't know where he is. And I wish you would trust me. I don't know what's going on with both of you in the streets, but whatever it is, I want out of it."

"As long as you're my wife, you don't have that option. You're either on my side or you're dead."

"Cage..."

He lowered his brow. "You still care about him, don't you?"

"All I want is for him to be happy just like I want the same for you."

"The difference is, I'm your husband. Fuck you care about his happiness for?" He yanked her, squeezing hard.

Any angrier he would've broken her arms.

"Cage you're hurting me."

"I'll do worse if I catch you with that nigga. Do you hear me?"

"Cage, please."

Slowly he released her and wondered if this was the Vamp Rage Arabia told him about. "I'm sorry. I didn't mean to--"

"Are you? Because it hasn't felt like you care much about anything lately." She walked closer. "What is happening right now? Do you have plans for him or something?"

"All I'm going to say is this, keep your distance. And if I find out you are seeing him, you're dead."

Arabia walked into a massive black church, where the Vampire Elders sat, waiting on her to enter.

When she came through the door, she could feel their eyes upon her body.

By T. Styles

Sitting on the stage as they sat in the audience, she took a deep breath. "I'm here."

"What's happening, Arabia?" Viking asked.

"He's coming around."

Viking stood up and looked directly into her eyes. "We need him to either get on the throne or get out of the way so we can find another. The Wolves' cravings are awakening. And if we're going to sacrifice part of The Collective, to save ourselves, we have to do it now. Talk to him. Get him to do what's necessary. I'm depending on you."

CHAPTER NINE
"This offer expires."

Cage and Row were on the court playing basketball.

Cage was surprised at how good Row was until he remembered his mother telling him that Magnus could also ball.

After making a shot, Cage grabbed the ball and took a deep breath. "I think you need to get your pack together more than ever, Row. You need to convince them to follow your lead."

"Not that I owe you any explanation, but we already doing that."

Cage bounced the ball and took a shot. "That's good."

"But why you so interested?"

"Onion's causing problems. Right now, his actions are geared toward me. But it's just a matter of time before he drags the Wolves into his games with his lies. Since I have Wolves in my family."

"We'll be unified. I already set up a meeting."

"More than unified. You'll have to be able to control the packs. To calm them down if they are riled up for any reason. Things are about to get heavy."

By T. Styles

Flow had just lost ten thousand dollars via an online betting site. Lying face up in bed, he hit his brother's phone number once more.

He needed his cash.

"Are you good?" Cage asked right off the bat.

"I want my money."

"Do you want me to pay a bill? Put a down payment on your own crib?"

"It's my money, Cage. Give it to me."

"I know what it is. And it'll be given to you based on the terms of your trust. I dropped the papers off to you a few days ago. Look it over and let's talk."

Flow was getting agitated.

Having Cage control his money was bothersome, especially since he wanted to make gambling moves. Call it an excuse, but he was tired of begging.

"You know what, fuck it." He ended the call.

Picking up the phone again, he dialed the red number on the black card Onion gave him and sighed.

Seconds later he answered.

"I've been waiting for you to call."

Flow sat up. "That's a bit strange but whatever."

"What you want to do?"

Flow rose and walked over to the edge of the room. "I'm ready to take you up on your offer."

"What changed?"

Flow readjusted his dick. "Does it matter?"

Onion laughed once. "It's not that it matters but I wanna know all the same."

"Cage is in charge of my money. And he has yet to divvy it out to me or my siblings. He's probably spending my shit as we speak."

"I wouldn't be surprised."

"Not asking you to be surprised or not. Anyway, until he gives me my paper, I gotta get paid through other means."

"So that's where I come in?"

"Pretty much."

"Let's do this, how about we meet."

"When?"

"Tonight."

"I can't tonight." He dragged a hand down his face. "Let's make it tomorrow."

"Don't make me wait too long. This offer expires."

Earlier that night, Onion pulled up to the abandoned restaurant and Angelina wasn't there.

He was trying to be patient but seeing her the two times had him wanting more. And not getting her back on his leash by now made him more focused than ever on bringing Cage down.

So, he pulled up to a busy college instead.

Rolling down his window when he saw a group of girls, he focused on the one with the red dress. Besides, based on odors she gave off the fruitiest scent. Which meant she was the closest to not having respect or love for herself.

"Can I take you wherever you're about to go?"

She started to say no, until she turned around and noticed Onion's luxurious car and handsome face.

By T. Styles

She loved what she saw.

"Damn, girl," the one with the tight jeans said to her homie. "He fine as fuck. You got any friends?" She asked him.

"Right now, the only friend I'm interested in is yours." He focused on Red Dress. "You riding with me?"

"You better." Tight Jeans said. "If you don't, I will."

Onion smiled.

"What's your name?" Tight Jeans asked, as if he hadn't made clear who he wanted to meet. "Since you taking my friend and all."

"Cage. Cage Stryker." He looked at Red Dress. "You riding or not?"

"I don't see why not." She shrugged.

"Yes or no?"

"Yes." Red Dress giggled, as she quickly got into his car and locked her door. "Where we going?"

As Onion passed her friends, he pulled up about a mile down the way. The once charismatic man now was deathly silent.

"Hello, where are we going?"

He looked at her and focused back on the road.

"You know what, let me out." When she moved to leave, he held her with one hand and pulled into the alley.

"Get off me!" She yelled.

When he opened his mouth and his fangs dropped, she was scared silent. "Who are you? What...what are you doing?"

Leaning over he pulled her toward him and bit down into her neck, before draining her dry.

He was certain that her friends would give Cage Stryker's name and that once again, he would appear to be losing control.

Which eventually would push him out of favor with the Elders.

But more importantly, Angelina.

The sun was going down on Row and his brothers' home, as they stood in front of their niece and nephews.

This was the moment that Row and his brothers had been waiting on and at the same time they were greatly concerned. Because they knew that introducing Magnus' sons and daughter would bring with it certain expectations.

And while they knew Tatum, being the oldest, should be the next to lead the packs, they couldn't be certain that he was ready. He seemed far too interested in his video games and online presence than he did leading.

Even the uncles varied on what needed to happen for the future of the pack.

Row believed Magnus' spawns were the answer. While Canelo, who peeped how the nephews moved, believed they were far from ready.

Standing in front of Bloom, Tatum and Flow, Row took a deep breath. "This meeting is very serious tonight." He looked each of them in the eyes. "You'll

By T. Styles

get more of an understanding than you ever have before of what we're about. And I want you to suspend your beliefs but at the same time understand that for us uniting the packs is all we care about. The tighter we are, the higher our chances for survival."

"Uncle, what do you want from us? When we get there?" Bloom asked.

"For now, all I want is for you and your brothers to get inundated with the way we do things. Study our culture. We've waited far too long for this moment and now it's arrived."

"What do you want us to say?" Tatum question.

"Nothing. After the introductions we will field all questions. More than anything I want you to pay attention. I want them to know Magnus' children are the future."

Row noticed that while Bloom and Tatum seemed concerned and eager to put on a good face, Flow appeared indifferent. It was as if his mind was elsewhere.

"Flow, do you have any questions?" Row pushed.

"Nah." He shrugged. "Not really."

"Well, I'm going to prepare everyone in the auditorium now." Row continued. "I expect you all to be on time."

When the uncles left Tatum looked at Bloom and Flow. "What do you think will happen tonight?" Tatum asked. "Because it's like they're expecting something to happen that we don't know anything about."

"Didn't he just say we don't have to do nothing?" Flow responded.

"Why does everything have to be a fight with you lately?" Bloom asked. "He just asking a question."

"Because I don't feel like going to no meeting. I don't feel like faking in front of a bunch of people I don't even know. All I want is my money."

"And Cage said he will give it to us." She spoke.

"Give it to us when though?!" Flow yelled. "Don't you see what he's doing? He has this massive home while we're living--"

"In luxury." Tatum interrupted. "I mean Cage's house is sweet and I love it there. He wanted you to stay too but you chose to live with the uncles."

"That's just it, it's Cage's house. Not yours!"

"He gave us enough money to buy a place that we can afford. Stop trying to tear us apart." Tatum responded. "Let's go, Bloom. This nigga tripping."

They both walked out leaving Flow alone.

The meeting Row and his brothers held with the leaders of the major packs was loud and rowdy.

There were over 100 wolves present and they all had their opinions on how the packs should be run.

The older packs tended to rule based on morals, honor, and code.

While the younger packs were more concerned with dope money, dick, pussy, and trouble.

Right on time Bloom and Tatum walked through the door of the auditorium. Although a few of the pack leaders looked at them when they entered, for the most part they continued to speak loudly.

This tension happened whenever the packs got together. And it was the main reason Row solicited Cage for his nephews and niece.

At the end of the day, Magnus' children were their last hope.

But when they walked inside, no respect was given.

"I told you this wouldn't work," Canelo whispered to Row as Bloom and Tatum approached the stage.

"It's not over yet." Row hoped.

"They didn't even look their way when they walked inside. You know packs can sense alphas. This was a bad move."

"Well what else can we do?" Row continued. "We're at the point where we have to try something different. We'll be dead or at war with the Vampires if shit don't change soon."

Bloom and Tatum joined their side.

The uncles nodded to them, and Row took the mic.

"Settle down everyone!" He raised his hands. "I have some very important people I want you to meet!"

"We already know who them niggas are," Gunnar said from the crowd. His pack ran out of the city, and they were the most disrespectful of the young packs to date. "But what we don't get is what you expect them to do for us! From the beginning all we've been hearing is that the wealth will be shared amongst the packs! When all I see are the older packs getting paper off our backs!"

There were many cheers in agreement with him.

"This is what this meeting is about!" Row yelled. "It's time for us to come together. To come to an understanding. When we do that, we will also earn together."

The room grew louder and more ignorant as the Elders tried desperately to squeeze out the last bit of respect from the young'uns.

It wasn't working.

"Settle down!" Row yelled. "There will come a time very soon where we will be plucked off if we don't unite! And if we don't, we will all remember this night."

Bloom and Tatum looked at one another concerned.

"It's happening to The Vamps already. It will happen to us next."

"Is that why you keeping time with a Vamp right now?" Gunnar asked sarcastically. "So, you can turn on us and save yourselves?"

Tatum and Bloom looked at each other knowing full well they were talking about Cage.

"What I'm saying is we can no longer last or survive if we continue on the way we are going. Not to mention, we're bringing excessive attention our way. If the Norms find out, fear will take over and we will be hunted."

More loud talk.

Zero respect.

Fuck the packs. Row thought.

He was about to start knocking young nigga's heads off their shoulders until Flow walked inside. Unlike when his sister and brother entered, everybody turned in his direction.

Fifteen minutes late, it suddenly didn't matter.

By T. Styles

Because the way he moved towards the stage was with extreme confidence and swagger.

Despite being angry, he knew who he was and so he immediately claimed respect.

As he made his way slowly to the stage, Flow's eyes rested on several pack leaders. It was as if he was saying with his eyes, *"I wish a wolf would..."*

This nigga wanted a fight, and it was clear he was willing to battle to the death. Just like Wolves in the wild, out of respect, they readjusted their stares and looked the other way.

They didn't want the heat.

And Row and Canelo caught the temperature change, and it almost took their breath away.

"It's him." Row whispered to Canelo with a smile on his face. "It's him."

As Flow bopped up to the podium and stood next to his siblings there was not a voice or comment made in the room.

It was deathly silent.

That moment for Row was official.

To him, Flow was king.

But Canelo thought otherwise.

PRESENT DAY
"Why didn't you touch me?"

Violet didn't want the night with Pierre to end.

As the chauffeured luxury vehicle strolled down the road on the way to her house, she was disappointed. After all, despite being a good girl she wanted a bit more from Pierre.

Instead, she was more embarrassed by her thirst because Pierre appeared not to want to take things to the next level.

Did she say something to turn him off?

Positioning herself to look directly at him she said, "I don't mean to be weird but tonight was one of the best nights of my life. And even though I just met you at the coffee shop, I wanted more."

He winked. "I'm happy to hear that, beautiful."

Her head tilted to the left. "Are you really though?"

"Of course, I am. Why would you question that?"

She shrugged. "It just seemed that you weren't interested. At one-point things were going smooth and then...I don't know. Maybe I'm looking into things too deeply, but you were in a rush to drop me off quickly."

He stared at her with confusion. "Violet, it seems as if we're going to have to retrace the steps leading up to this moment."

"I don't get it."

"As far as I remember, my day started like this. I came into the coffee shop, and I ended up meeting one of the most beautiful and intelligent women I've ever met in my life. We left for dinner. She declined

104   By T. Styles

dinner and I showed her the most sacred place in my home instead. Now we're here. So, if you saw anything other than me being extremely interested, it's definitely my fault."

"You're just saying that." She looked down.

"We've just met each other. Have I treated you in any way that would make you think that I'm a liar?"

She was so used to fucking with losers that she didn't consider the garbage flying out of her mouth.

"Of course, you haven't done anything to make me think that."

"Then when I tell you I'm feeling you, I'm asking that you believe me."

"So why didn't you touch me? At all tonight."

"I'm more interested in why you feel a man needs to be physical with you in order to display your worth to him. I mean, I could've grabbed the back of your head and whipped out my dick, but that would have immediately messed up your image of me."

Okay, now she wanted to crawl up under the car with the hope that at least the back tires would roll her over.

"It's not that it's just--"

"Unless you think otherwise, I intend on being a staple in your life my Sweet Violet. I had a long night and so I wanted to make sure I retire without sleeping on you."

"Do you mean inside of me?" Suddenly she reached over and pressed her lips against his.

Nothing.

His mouth was as stiff as a board.

Her attempts to be sexy didn't land.

And again, she wanted to crawl up under the car.

"I'm sorry, Pierre. I shouldn't have done that."

"We will have plenty of time to get to know one another in that way. But when that happens, I don't want it to be some desperate fuck on the way to your house."

"Desperate?"

Silence.

"Wow." She sighed.

"I didn't mean it that way. I want to reintroduce your body to you through my eyes." He positioned himself so that he could look at her square on. "But not now."

"I don't understand."

"I want you to see the beauty I see when I look at you. And then I want you to feel me. Like I want to feel you. Violet, with all of the things I imagined doing to you, as erotic as it will be, none of them entail fucking you in the backseat of a car."

Welp.

He said what he said.

As the vehicle pulled up to her house, she noticed her sister's pink Range Rover in front of her condominium. She let out a large sigh in annoyance.

"You good?"

"Yes...I'm...I'm fine."

Pierre exited his car and opened her door. Standing in front of her when she looked down, he softly raised her chin so that she was looking up into his eyes.

"Slow, Miss Violet. I promise it'll be worth the wait."

She smiled.

What else could she do?

It wasn't like she was getting the dick *soooooo*.

He attempted to walk her to her house but the last thing she needed was her sisters who she was sure were sitting in her living room as if they owned the place ruining it all.

"I'll be fine."

He winked. "I'll sit right here until I see the door open, and you go inside."

She nodded and took the long road to the entrance before disappearing.

The moment she crossed her threshold, the drama began.

"Who was that man?" Chloe asked with her hands on her hips.

Violet looked at Jeanette, who was nice to her when they were alone. But she turned to a mean and violent person when she was with Chloe.

"Why are y'all in my house?" Violet rolled her eyes and tossed her purse on the end table. Walking to the sofa she popped off her shoes. "Plus, who I'm seeing is none of your fucking business."

Both of her sisters stood in front of her in awe that she was snapping.

"What did the lawyer say?" Chloe asked. "No fucking games."

They were talking about the attorney earlier who all but explained that she was the sole heir to their grandmother's multimillion-dollar estate. She hadn't planned it to be this way and yet here she was virtually independently wealthy.

"It doesn't matter." She flopped on her sofa.

"That's not what we asked you." Chloe said.

"Just tell her, Violet. Damn. Why make it harder?"

Any other time Violet would have been scared.

After all, that was Violet's nature to let others take advantage of her when she wanted to say more. But she felt a type of way tonight now that Pierre's sexy ass noticed her.

"He told me that I'm the sole heir to Abuela's estate."

The sisters looked at one another and then back down at her.

"What you talking about?" Chloe yelled. "You ain't the only blood relative."

"I don't know what you want me to say. But I'll put it like this. You (clap hands) not (clap hands) getting (clap hands) shit. That's Abuela's request." She snapped her fingers.

As the broke sisters looked upon one another they silently decided at that moment, to take what was theirs.

And unfortunately for Violet things wouldn't end well. Because they took to doing something they could never undo.

"What about the stipend she gives you every month?" Chloe said. "You can at least break us off with some of that shit."

"That money is mine too."

"Is it really though?" She tied up her hair.

As Jeanette closed the curtains, Chloe kicked off her shoes and cracked her knuckles.

Standing directly in front of Violet she now realized the length her sisters would go to get at the cash. Because that night, they beat her within every inch of her life.

CHAPTER TEN
"I'm quite aware of our fucking future!"

Cage picked up Langley from his house. The moment he saw his face he knew what he was about to say before he said the words.

"I met up with Berg like you said. Kept the press on them and everything, but Onion is doing a good job of hiding the people who roll with him."

He sighed. "That's fine. I shouldn't have charged you with that."

"The one you call Cheddar; do you know if he's a day walker?"

"He's full Vamp. And he was Tino's right hand."

He sighed. "I'm sorry to let you down, boss."

"You haven't. This was a lot to put on you. I got one last trick up my sleeve. Don't worry, shit will work out."

Onion and Cheddar were in a private Vamp club. Although Cheddar was desperately trying to restore Onion's image, Onion didn't seem too keen on looking the part.

"Why you got me in this bougie ass club wearing cologne and shit?" He asked, sipping the blood in his cup doused with a little wine.

"I want people to see who you really are."

Onion frowned. "As opposed to what?"

"You haven't heard?"

"Why everything gotta be a puzzle with you? What the fuck is going on?"

"Word has gotten around that you're a rapist."

Onion's eyes widened and he dropped the cup on the table. Blood splattered everywhere.

Good thing he was dressed in black.

"A... a rapist? Who the fuck started that shit?"

"I'm not sure. But a few people who I know made me believe that they were working with Cage."

"So, Cage did this shit to me?"

"Why you mad, nigga? Ain't you running around town sucking bitches on the necks and blaming him?"

"This shit different."

"It always is with you. That's your fucking problem." He paused. "Anyway, I don't think he would put a word out like that about you. I could be wrong, but I think he may still have a code. But the nigga he's dealing with don't give a fuck about shit. I believe his name is Berg."

Onion was heated and he would remember his name.

The only thing this made him want to do was go harder.

"And why are we here again?"

"Because when this war kicks off, I want people to see you in this element. I want them to know you can be refined."

"So, you want me to move like you?"

"What's better than imitating a nigga like me?"

Arabia walked into the lounge upon Cage's call. Standing in front of him she crossed her arms over her chest and took a deep breath. "You asked me to come quickly so what do you need?"

"I have a request."

She shook her head no.

"You don't even know what it is and yet you stand in front of me with an attitude?"

Now that was funny to Arabia.

"I am older than your mother would have been had she survived. My parents come from a long line of Vampires who roamed the earth before you were even thought of. And yet you would deduce how I feel down to two words like I'm a hood rat? *An attitude*?"

"Then what was that look?"

She stepped closer. "That look was because I'm tired of you thinking about the past. I've spoken with the Elders and things are getting dangerous, Cage. Stories of women getting bit on the neck are increasing. Bodies are being drained and left in the street. And in my opinion, you aren't putting your focus in the appropriate places. If this continues to happen, sitting on the throne will be the least of your worries. The Elders may put a blood bounty on your head that will be carried through. So, I beg you, leave the past alone."

He glared. "You questioned my interest in the past, when isn't all of this about the past? The legacy of the Vamps and how they've evolved over the years?"

"You know what I mean."

"Actually, I don't. There's somebody out there right now walking the earth who killed my father. And to make matters worse my siblings believe I was responsible."

"I don't know about Onion, but you could do something about your family to smooth things over. After all, why haven't you told them Onion was responsible?"

"Because you know that at the age they are right now, they would attempt to avenge my father's death. And I can't have anything happening to them."

"Okay, why am I here, Cage? Because you obviously don't want to talk about what I want to know."

"I will when you tell me where Onion is located. And I know you know."

"I do."

His fangs dropped. "Then why haven't you told me?"

"Because that's not the focus of our future."

"I'm quite aware of our fucking future!" He yelled.

"Are you? Do you understand how dangerous things will be for Norms if the Wolves and Vamps connect right now because they aren't controlled? More stories will begin to appear in the paper about people being sucked dry. Or even worse...of Vampire bodies in the middle of the street. The war will happen, but it has to be controlled."

"Where is he?" He stood up and walked toward her. "And I'm tired of having to ask you over and over again."

"I won't tell you." She stepped back. "And although you may look upon that as disrespect, I pray that in the future you see things my way.

She rushed towards the door and then he said, "I won't forget this. Even if I never say another word about it, I will remember the night you turned your back on me." He paused. "So, tell me the real reason."

"The real reason what?"

"The real reason you won't give me what I need to know."

"Because as it stands right now, because you took his woman, Onion is more suited for war than you are. He's angrier. And if you battle, you will lose."

She walked away.

Onion sat in his car looking at the news on his cell phone. Due to his bad deeds, several women were found dead in the middle of the street, with fang holes in their necks.

And to think, this was all his handy work.

He didn't care what could happen once the world knew of their existence.

Instead, he smiled when he realized what would happen when he unleashed his future army on the streets.

Cage would be dead.

And Angelina would be in his bed.

Taking a deep breath, totally satisfied, he walked into the club.

The club was packed with young Wolves and young Vamps.

The Wolves were all taller and stronger. The male Wolves' bodies were rocked up as if they were fresh out of prison. While the women had thick asses, strong legs, and B cup sized breasts.

The Vamps were another story.

They wore designer clothing, and most were dipped in diamonds, gold, and silver. Independently wealthy, their money was what a lot of Wolves lusted after the most.

And then there were the Norms, who were all struggling to get their attention while being totally unaware of their existence.

As the music pounded, fifteen young Wolves surrounded Flow as they stood in the nightclub. In a section designated for just the pack it was obvious that they were all somebody.

As Flow drank liquor and moved his head to the music, one of the young pack leaders turned his way. "There's a reason you invited us out." Gunnar asked.

"We'll get into business later." Flow waved the air. Shit would be done on his time and not sooner.

"Sure thing," he said. "Just didn't want to waste any of your time, that's all." He cleared his throat. "So, tell us about the great Magnus."

Flow gave him his undivided attention. "What about him?"

"Row and Canelo put on as if he was a king. Like everybody would have dropped to their knees just to be in his presence."

"That would be accurate." He paused. "You gotta problem with that or something?"

Gunnar resituated a little for fear he had disrespected a man who appeared to be the next thing coming. "I didn't mean it like that."

"Then what did you mean it like? Because what it's like now is that you talk too fucking much."

Gunnar nodded. "My bad."

As the male Wolves cowardly tried to get a position in his life one person stood in the corner of it all and remained silent. She had almond-shaped eyes, light brown skin and beautiful locked hair that ran down the middle of her back.

She was stacked the way he liked too.

'A' cup breasts.

A tiny waist.

A large ass that presented her body in an hourglass shape.

And she made her way in his direction without an invitation. "So, what do you have to say for yourself?" Flow asked her directly.

"If I wanted to speak, I would have talked already."

Flow was turned on.

The Wolves gasped and laughed before he glanced at them, which silenced them instantly.

"Your name?" Flow asked her.

"I don't know if I want you to have it just yet."

She was playing a game.

A dangerous one at that.

Her name was Mink and none of the other packs were surprised about anything she let fly out of her thick lips. She often didn't bite her tongue and as a result got on certain people's nerves who felt like she should know her position.

But she was just what Flow needed.

Just what he liked.

"Get over here." Flow said.

"No."

More people gasped.

Now she was on fickle ground, and she had better move carefully. Being embarrassed by the pack wasn't going to be tolerated well by Flow. If she was the right one, she would know this.

"If I have to get out of my seat and snatch you, I may ruin your night. So do as I say. Now."

Some people would have looked at the scenario as if he was being a bit abusive, but they were Wolves.

And Wolves played rough.

Besides, she loved every bit.

As her thick legs moved slowly in his direction she stood before him.

"Sit down." He didn't wait for her to make her move; he tugged her hard enough for her to lose balance and find her way on his dick.

"You're cocky." She smiled. "But I like it."

"Enjoy the spotlight," he told her. "It looks good on you."

Flow found his match.

Now it was time to take over.

CHAPTER ELEVEN
"At least there's loyalty."

Arabia and Cage sat in the back of a black van which seated eight. And yet with the exception of the driver, they were alone.

"I need you to understand what will take place tonight." Arabia started.

All he wanted was Shane and Ellis to be free. But he would give her the moment. "Why do I get the impression that you think I'm a child?"

"It's not that I think you are a child. As I've said many times before, at this point you are important for the cause, Cage. And doing something like this which seems more in line with revenge than anything else in my opinion is a waste of time. I wish you would've just stayed home. And let the men do the work."

"I can't do that."

"But why?"

"There was a point where I wasn't sure if I would ever be able to find my siblings. Shane and Ellis put their lives on the line for me. And I'm not going to reward them by turning my back on them. It's been too long already."

"At least there's loyalty."

"All there is, is loyalty."

"I know you're taking a shot at me, Cage. And I assure you that my loyalty lies with you, even if you believe differently." She took a deep breath. "But this will not end well."

"We have at least forty men. That should be enough."

"Even with that amount of manpower not everybody will be able to make it inside. You have to remember this property is gated and secured. Savannah made sure before she died."

"But it's a hair factory."

"It's not about it being a hair factory. This is a front for Savannah's roofie operation which is run by her cousins. First it was all about the drugs. After some time, since wigs & hair extensions were big business, she continued to operate them both at the same time. But drugs were always her focal point. That hasn't stopped since you took her life. Her cousins will have men armed and ready at the gates to protect their product, even in her death."

"And you sure Shane and Ellis are inside? Because if they are, it's whatever."

"The last I heard they were."

"Then we getting up in that bitch."

Fifteen minutes later Cage and Arabia's van parked alongside the dark road toward the left of the property. When the vehicle came to a halt, Cage hopped out and approached one of the four vans that also parked out of the camera's view.

Standing before them, he looked at everyone individually. "Not everybody will make it tonight. But trust, if something happens, all of your families will be taken care of." With those words he looked at the building which moonlighted as a hair manufacturing company and said, "Let's follow the plan."

Jim and three other security guards stood at the gate surrounding the property smoking weed. Although if Savannah was alive, she never would have stood for such fuckery; not much went down at the facility after her death.

And as a result, most of them were comfortable.

"So yeah, she wants me to sign divorce papers." Jim said.

"Just do it."

"So, she can get a child support check too? Nah, I'm good."

"Well, you have to do something. Because she's going to keep hounding you if you don't."

Jim stared into the distance. "Wait, what's that?" He saw some figures moving.

Quickly all three guards focused on the direction, but it was too late. Before they knew it the gates came down and Cage's men breached the line.

Once the gate was destroyed and the guards were shot, they approached every door surrounding the property with fury.

Knocking three times which was the code, one of Savannah's men allowed them inside as they eventually met their demise. Using all of his manpower, the moment Cage's people made it across the threshold guns fired from every direction toward them.

They fired back but like Arabia said, this was not going to be an easy battle.

Because on the first level alone six armed men shot at Cage's men as they fired rounds at them in defense. It was clear that this battle was going to be won by the team with the most bullets and the coldest gunplay.

Five minutes later three of Cage's eight men remained but luckily, he came prepared and so he waved more inside.

The fight went on for fifteen minutes as they encountered gun play on every level.

In the end, after twenty of his crew were murdered, surprisingly, his men were able to overtake the building.

But where was Shane and Ellis?

After a lot of searching, Cage happened upon one last door. It was the only entryway that hadn't opened since it all began.

"This one remained locked," one of his men whispered.

They were inside.

He felt it in his heart.

Curious, Cage pushed past the men and grabbed the knob turning lightly.

Towards the far back were Shane, who was also named Pigsty and Ellis who had a hazy cornea. They both lost between fifteen to twenty pounds and looked hard.

They didn't see him at first. Besides, they were too busy bagging drugs.

There were two armed men on the right and left of them to ensure that things went smoothly.

The guards saw Cage and his crew when it was too late.

120   By T. Styles

Cage's men quickly aimed ten barrels in their direction, but Savannah's remaining guards were ready.

To prevent the heat, Cage raised his hand.

When Shane and Ellis focused on the disruption, they saw their old friend. And they couldn't believe their eyes.

After so many years, he actually found them.

Focusing on the men around his friends he said, "All I want is Shane and Ellis. Nothing less nothing more. Give them to me and I'll let you go."

"Why should we believe you?" One of them asked with the gun shivering in his hand.

"I don't care if you believe me or not, nigga! What I know is this, you won't make it out of here alive if either one of them are harmed. Fuck y'all wanna do?"

CHAPTER TWELVE
"We home now."

Hours later, Cage, Shane and Ellis sat in Cage's lounge drinking wine.

"How did you know where we were?" Shane said, his hand visibly shaking. He couldn't believe he was home.

Cage didn't want to tell them that Arabia hid the information the whole time, because he knew they would never fuck with her in the future.

He sighed. "At first I thought you were dead. Both of you. But something didn't sit right with me. I kept asking around, trying to find more information and nothing. After a while, I learned about the warehouse."

Ellis took a deep breath. "That bitch...Savannah, tortured us. For years. Even when she died it was like they kept doing shit to us, just because those were the final orders she gave them before you killed her ass."

"How have things been for you?" Ellis asked. "You look good."

"Compared to what y'all been through, shit been straight."

"We asking because we want to know," Shane said. "So, talk to us."

Cage felt like a bitch complaining from his ivory tower, especially considering what they went through, but shit was on his mind.

"It's been rough mainly because I can't trust anybody around me. Not even my own family members."

They looked at one another.

Before they even told him what he didn't want to hear he already knew what they were about to say.

"You don't have to say it." Cage said, taking a sip.

"It's not that we don't want to be a part of your collection. It's just that we have to get to our families and--"

"Like I said, you don't have to say anything, brother," he said, cutting Ellis off. "Seriously. I'm happy you're alive and safe. And I'm sorry it took me so long to find you. It's--"

"Let me finish." Ellis interrupted. "We need to go see our families and then we need to have eyes for you in the daytime. If we're a part of your collection, we can't do that."

"Yeah, man." Shane said. "We know you got a new wife. And we're happy that worked out. But she won't be able to do what's needed. We will."

They were right.

He barely trusted her when he could see her face.

"Taking The Fluid, as fun as it would be, will limit us." Ellis continued. "That means it would limit you too."

Cage knew they were right, but it still fucked him up. In his firm opinion having them in his collection would make him deadly. He knew they would ride for him. They did it all the way up to being snatched by Savannah.

"What made her snatch you?" He asked, looking between them. "Talking about Savannah."

Shane and Ellis looked at one another.

"One night she asked us how we feel about working with you. We got the impression that she wanted us to turn our backs on you. To make a long story short we didn't take the bait. And she rewarded us by getting us snatched."

Cage shook his head.

"One thing this shit has taught us is to be careful," Ellis said rubbing his hazy eye.

"He's right, nobody will ever catch us slipping again," Shane continued. "And that means nobody will catch you slipping either. We home now."

Cage was sipping blood in his bedroom when he heard commotion outside of his door.

"Cage, I think the police are here," Bloom yelled.

"The police?"

His eyes widened as he approached the bedroom door and pulled it open. He was basically off the grid, so how did they find him? More importantly, what the fuck did they want?

Rushing down the hallway, Bloom was hot on his trail. "We gonna have to move if I survive this shit. Go to your room."

"But what's going on?"

"Go!"

When she left, he took a deep breath and pulled the front door open, "How can I help you?"

Two white officers stood in front of him, with no nonsense looks on their faces.

"Are you Cage Stryker?"

"I am."

By T. Styles

"May we come inside?"

They smelled of burnt cookies, and he would have drained them both dry if it meant he could survive.

He opened the door wider but paused in his foyer. They didn't need to go any further in his home.

"What do you want?"

"We can do this at the station in the morning if it's more convenient."

They were saying it to be sarcastic, and yet Cage knew if he ever had to go to the station in the morning, his life would be over. And his secret would be out.

"I have time right now."

"There have been a series of young women being left on the streets over the past week. And one thing that keeps coming up is your name. Cage Stryker. Do you know anything about that?"

"Women left on the streets?" He heard all about it but faked dumb.

"Yes. Dead."

Cage's jaw twitched. "Nah. I don't know anything. I don't follow the news much."

"Well, you haven't heard the worst. There are claims of Vampires too. And unless we are in a fucking fantasy world, we all know there is no such thing. And still, we had to come here to ask questions."

"Like I said, I don't know of any dead women. And I'm not sure why my name is coming up in the mix."

They nodded. "You have something red on your lips. Is it blood?" He joked.

It was blood.

"That would be something else wouldn't it?" Cage laughed.

Cage wiped it off coolly, careful not to raise any alarms.

"Is there anything else?" Cage crossed his arms.

The officer looked up at the vaulted ceilings and the chandeliers before focusing back on him. "What do you do for a living?"

"I inherited money from my father."

"Must be a nice life. Must be a good father."

"Not to be rude, but is there anything else?"

"No for now. We will be in contact."

Cage couldn't wait to get his hands on Onion. He literally blew up his spot, which put The Collective and his life in danger.

But first he had to make a few moves.

Angelina sat with her head hung low as Cage leaned up against the wall in their bedroom. He smelled clean and his skin glistened after just showering.

Damn she wanted him badly.

She handed him his red velvet robe. "So, what are you going to do? About the police?"

"Nothing right now."

"Do you know why they--."

"I have to get ready for tonight. I'm sorry but I can't talk about anything else right now."

She crossed her arms over her chest and then released them. "So, it's really about to happen?

By T. Styles

You're still creating a collection even though the police *just* showed up here?"

"We've talked about it already."

"Not really. You talked about it and just told me how it was going to be."

"And yet here we are."

"What does that mean, Cage?"

"It means that I'm tired of saying the same thing to you over and over again. This is my new life. And I want you to be a part of it."

"Then make me a part of your collection."

He glared. "Fuck is wrong with you? I can't do that! And this is the last time I'm going to have a conversation with you about what goes on behind those doors. You're my wife. I love you. But I have to do what I have to do." He kissed her on the cheek. "I'll get up with you later."

Candles flickered on the wall mounts, bringing with it an illuminating glow.

Just like Tino, Cage had a ceremony room in the basement of his mansion, and it was spectacular. The walls were covered with black Paisley and there was no unnatural lighting anywhere to be found.

The ceremony room was official.

Along with forty-nine Vampires needed to welcome fifty of Cage's upcoming members, the room was packed, and the atmosphere was perfect. The future Stryker Collection was excited as this had been the moment they were waiting on.

Cage, dressed in his robe that hung open, revealing his chiseled chest and *Magnus* chain, stood in front of the newcomers. While the forty-nine assistant Vamps hung behind him.

Cage would make the 50 necessary.

Helena's eyes sparkled with delight; she was so excited.

At that moment both of them knew that she would be the position for the evening. Being the position was a unique honor, because after Cage immersed his DNA with each of his new members, he would inevitably return back to her, to finish out the night.

In order to prepare for this event Arabia went all out. She had Cage drink plenty of liquids and put him on a diet of only the purest blood. Finding pure blood was difficult because it meant selecting individuals with clean diets.

And since most Norms with sweet smelling blood ate shitty food, it was extremely difficult.

But Arabia understood that in order to effectively create the Stryker Collection, he had to install his fluid at a higher rate than the forty-nine Vampires who were needed to assist and help them into the Vamp world.

The selected members of Cage's Collection were varied. Twenty-eight had the gene, and only needed The Fluid. While twenty-two needed the bite and The Fluid.

This would be a long night.

Even Arabia was there for the ceremony although some were unsure why she was present. Being a day

By T. Styles

walker, she couldn't contribute anything of value to the ceremony.

And yet there she was.

Gawking.

With the forty-nine behind him, Cage said, "After tonight everything will change. We will be connected in ways people can't imagine. Our unity and how we will operate, will be necessary to protect and keep each other safe. When you accept The Fluid, I pray that you honor us by respecting our motto too. *Control your urges. Control the flesh.*" Cage looked at the forty-nine. "And I thank you for trusting me by helping me usher fifty more into our world."

Cage focused back on Helena.

His dick hardened.

His fangs dropped.

"Shall we begin?"

All of the upcoming collection members laid down on the soft floor bed.

To begin the ceremony, first the forty-nine Vampires went around the room and kissed each member. The liquid was enough to fill up several cups. The men went to the female members of Cage's collection while the women Vampires went to the males. After kissing each, the forty-nine Vampires left the room, as their DNA was enough to start the process.

The rest was up to Cage.

The first place Cage went was to Helena.

She had the gene.

All she needed was The Fluid.

And she was ready.

It was a fact, the hornier the Vampires got, the more fluid could be generated.

Seduction was a part of the act.

Helena widened her legs. Her body appeared to soften as Cage eased on top of her. Kissing her profusely she began to feel dizzy under his kiss. His liquid was as sweet as honeysuckle syrup and just as deadly as it would be to humans.

But he wasn't making humans.

He was making bloodsuckers.

After moving in and out of her pussy, he filled her up with his sweet nectar. Damn that shit was right.

He could've stayed there all night.

But there was work to be done.

When he saw in her eyes that her body was responding to his liquid, he grinned.

Quickly he rose and entered another female with his semen. When he finished, he instructed one of the male members of his collection to suck, so that they would also be infused with his liquid.

One by one Cage came inside each woman and had every man in his collection share the juice.

This went on for two hours until the men and women of his collection began to moan as they had sex with one another.

Arabia may have pretended as if she wasn't enjoying the show, but Cage saw the way her legs squeezed together as she was undoubtedly pushing her inner thighs against her clit.

When they were done, instead of dropping into a deep sleep, Cage ordered everyone to rise.

Still a gentleman, he extended his hand to help Helena to her feet.

Arabia rose too, wondering what was happening. This was odd. Usually, Vampires would be so tired they would drift off to sleep.

So what was going on?

Walking to a rectangular type of box, he flipped the lid. Inside, a wooden knife laid on a red velvet pillow. He removed it and stood in front of them.

"Cage, what's going on?" Arabia asked.

"Are they welcome?" He asked, nodding to his collection.

"Cage, I'm confused."

"Are they welcome or not?" He said harder.

"Yes, but what's going on?"

Cage ignored the bitch and focused back on his collection. "If we are now connected, this will prove it." Slowly he dug the knife into his arm, opening his flesh. On sight each of them grabbed their flesh in the same position, indicating that they felt his pain.

Cage smiled.

It worked.

"Welcome to the world, Stryker Collection. Let me see your smile."

They grinned as their fangs dropped.

CHAPTER THIRTEEN
"Take your positions!"

Unlike Cage's, Onion's ceremony was some trash.

Needing a big space as well, he used the warehouse of one of his allies for his ceremony.

It took Cheddar a long time to find the forty-nine Vampires necessary to assist Onion in the conversion of his collection.

But after bribing with wine, blood and rank pussy, Cheddar got what they needed. Most of the assistant Vamps came from collections of owners who were dead. These sorts of Vamps were easier to convince.

Now it was time for the conversion of the O Collection to begin.

And unlike the civilized way in which Cage conducted his ceremony, this was strictly hood shit.

They had a blood party before the formalities. Wine bottles crashed against the ground as they gouged on the liquid.

It was all a mess.

After sucking blood from the inside thigh of a woman who was lying on the floor with her legs gaped open, Onion rose from her weakened flesh and wiped his mouth with the back of his hand.

He shoved a few of the Vampires who were needed to convert off of the necks of women who they were sucking, so that everyone could focus.

With the forty-nine half-drunk converters behind him and the members of his collection standing in front of him he said, "I know nobody respects us in The Collective. And after this conversion tonight, they

By T. Styles

will try to write us off. But that's the beauty about what we'll create together in this world. There will come a time where anybody who is not for us will be against us. And we will make them sorry. Their fear will fuel us more than blood. And this fear will make us powerful."

Everyone cheered.

Even the forty-nine Vampire assistants.

"Right now, nothing is more important than the Vamps in this room. The blood we will drink together. The money we will make together. And the bodies that will fall if anybody disrespects us on the way to building our empire."

They cheered again.

"I am an unlikely hero. The kind of person The Collective wishes didn't exist. I guess that makes me a villain and you are too!"

"Facts!" A future O collection member yelled.

"Say it again!" Another responded.

But he didn't say it again.

Instead, he raised his hand to silence them momentarily.

"Tonight, we will be connected in ways few will understand. But we don't give a fuck, do we?!"

Louder cheers.

"Now, lay down! Take your positions!"

His dick hardened and he shifted it to the right.

Slowly his fangs dropped.

Everyone hustled to fall in line.

"After tonight nothing will ever be the same!" Onion said, as he ran his tongue over the spikes of his fangs.

At first the forty-nine Vampire assistants kissed each member of the fifty. Afterwards they left.

Now it was Onion's turn.

One by one he filled up the women with his saliva and sperm, and the men followed behind to suck the nectar from their bodies.

For his position, Onion took a woman who reminded him so much of Angelina, he wanted to suck her dry.

Her name was Carmen.

And she was the same person Cage rejected at the club.

Now she would be a part of Onion's Collection.

After an epic orgy session, each member of the O Collection fell into a deep sleep.

While Onion stood against the wall and smiled.

Onion was busted after his ceremony but the next night he would sooner kill himself than to miss his position in front of the abandoned restaurant.

And so, slightly exhausted due to not getting his weight up the night before his collection ceremony, he was spent. And yet when he arrived at the spot, he was shocked to see Angelina already there.

He jumped out his ride so quickly, he almost forgot to put that bitch in park. He had to hit it back inside and pull the brake or his shit would've crashed.

With the wheels under control, he rushed in her direction before walking slowly. She met him halfway.

No words.

Just stares, as they looked at one another.

Breaking down she said, "I...I just need to talk. Take me somewhere. Anywhere. I don't care."

"I know a place."

That place was home.

He drove erratically but forty minutes later, while blindfolded, he took her to his house. It wasn't that he didn't trust her. He just didn't want to put her in a situation where if she were tortured, she would give up his location.

Once they were in his room, he removed the blindfold.

She was so stunned at what she saw she stumbled backwards.

Black framed photos of the times they shared together as kids were all over the walls. She could tell that he still adored her after all of these years. And it made her heart flutter.

"Onion...I...I don't get it. Don't you ever bring other women here?"

"No. Even if I did, none of them, not a one, could hold a position next to you."

Suddenly she broke down crying.

Over the next hour she expressed everything that wrecked her mind about Cage. How he wasn't present mentally. How he didn't find her attractive anymore.

Onion was so angry at the level of disrespect he showed her, that it had him plotting even worse fates for his once close friend than he previously imagined.

After all, wasn't this the same man who grew angry with him because he didn't treat her right?

"What should I do?" She asked as she lay in his bed, in his arms, fully clothed.

He could tell her to leave his ass, but this was the long con.

Shit had to be done right.

Take your time, Onion. He thought.

"You should sleep tonight. You should consider what you really want. And if it's him, make it work. If not, leave the nigga."

"Why, so you can be with me?"

He laughed once. "The love I have for you not going anywhere. Do I think you supposed to be mine? Yes. But I think you should be happy more than anything else."

His words were perfect.

How could she fight him on it?

"Can I have something to drink?"

He nodded and walked out the room. The moment he did he ran into Cheddar.

"Is you crazy, nigga?" He snapped, pointing at his bedroom door.

Onion glared. "You better watch your step."

"Watch my step? Nigga, it's 'cause of me you still breathing. And you bring the bitch who is five minutes from causing a war to the house?"

Onion dropped him.

It was a stiff fist to the jaw.

Slowly Cheddar rose.

"I'm a trash bag." Onion said. "I get it. I fuck and suck these bitches without giving a fuck if they live or die. But Angelina is different. The sooner you realize that the better off shit will be between us."

136

"And let me say something to you. The next time you hit me, will be the last time you breathe."

"I guess we know where each other stands."

Cheddar shook his head and walked away.

CHAPTER FOURTEEN
"You look like your father."

After the conversion Cage woke up exhausted. Arabia had warned him that hosting a fluid ceremony took a lot out of the body, but he didn't know fully what it meant until that moment.

When he rolled over in bed, he was surprised to see Angelina was not there.

"Angelina." He said softly.

Silence.

Easing out of bed he slipped into his black satin robe and yawned, "Angelina. Where are you?"

Walking through his house he saw Bloom and Tatum sitting at the table. They were having dinner even though for Cage this was considered the morning.

"Is it true that we're moving?" Bloom asked.

"Yeah, I can't have the police questioning me about shit every time a woman shows up missing."

"Did you do it?" Bloom questioned with widened eyes. "Did you take those women's blood? Because...because I understand if you did."

"No, he didn't do that shit!" Tatum said, nudging her silent.

Although Tatum heard one thing, Cage saw the twinkle in her eye from the mere idea of killing to satisfy one's urges.

She wanted to kill.

He decided that for now anyway, he wouldn't respond.

By T. Styles

But he was definitely worried about the baby Wolf.

Was Bloom awakening?

"Have you seen Angelina?" He walked to his fridge, which was different from theirs as it was all black and grabbed a fresh cup of blood.

Bloom looked at her brother and then at Cage. "Yeah."

His eyebrows rose. "Well, where is she?"

"She...she didn't come home last night."

"Meaning?"

"I haven't seen her all day."

Cage sat his cup down and scratched his head.

This type of behavior was unlike her, and he was somewhat worried. He decided to hit her phone. But all calls went unanswered and found a place in her voicemail. He didn't bother to leave a message.

Besides, if she was fine they both knew what he wanted.

For him to know where the fuck she was.

And better yet, was she sharing Onion's bed.

Arabia was sitting on his patio when Cage approached. Despite the anger etched on his face, he was still perfect in her eyes.

"Your ceremony was a success." She smiled. "And I can't get over how much you look like your father."

"Since it's impossible for me to look like Magnus I take it you're talking about Tino."

"Who else?" She laughed.

He had many questions, but he decided to ask one he never thought of before. "What kind of man was he?"

"I didn't think you wanted to know."

"I'm not sure I want to know now. But I'm asking anyway."

She sighed deeply. "Tino was complicated. And yet he did have rules and boundaries he wasn't willing to compromise for anyone."

"You expect me to believe that the man who ordered my father murdered had boundaries?"

"Not everything is black and white, Cage. Pretty soon you'll find out for yourself when you begin to lead."

He was done talking about what didn't matter. "I've done what you asked. And even though I do understand the reason for starting my collection, I'm done compromising. Where is Onion? I'm afraid he might have Angelina."

"And I already told you I can't give you that information."

"Even if it will help save me from doing something violent to innocent people?"

"Do you believe in prophecy?"

Of course, he didn't.

"Cage, what needed to happen to Magnus, I'm speaking of his death, needed to happen for you to fulfill your destiny. So had it been by Tino's hand or Onion's he would have died anyway."

She walked away.

And he was starting to hate her guts.

Canelo sniffed the air and could smell the exotic odor of meat he hadn't tasted in his home. When he bent the corner in his living room, he saw the source of the odor.

"We have to talk." Cage said standing up from the sofa.

"Hadn't expected this."

"Why?"

"Most people come to see Row. You know that and I know it too. I'm usually an afterthought."

Cage sat down again. "For what I'm about to say, I don't think he will help me."

"I'm listening."

He looked at him seriously. "I need you to find Onion."

"Before we talk about why, what's going on with you and Flow?"

He frowned. "He hasn't told you?"

"I don't know anything. I do know we had our meeting not too long ago with all of the packs. And they bowed down to him. Based on that it's just a matter of time before he takes complete control."

"You don't seem happy. Wasn't that the plan when y'all took me to that library?"

"I'm not sure that he's ready. Neither is Shannon."

"I believe you want to say something else but you're choosing to beat around the bush. I wish you wouldn't waste my time." Cage paused. "What do you want to know about Flow? Because truthfully, I haven't said two words to him since he tried to kill me. And I'm not exaggerating."

"No, I believe you. The smell Vampires are giving off is suddenly becoming, well, erotic."

Cage wouldn't dare tell him about how they would crave Vamp flesh in the future.

But did he know already?

"Can Flow be trusted?" Canelo asked.

"What I will say is this, when we were growing up, he had a weird habit. Sniffing seats belonging to women and--."

"We all did that." He chuckled once.

"Killing animals too? Because that was also his thing."

"Not killing animals for sport. But even that is not too far from a Wolf's nature."

"Well other than that, I believe Flow has a habit. My team caught him going to casinos and spending lots of money when I had him followed. That was the reason I put his cash in the trust. I would've given Bloom and Tatum access to their funds anyway, but I didn't want Flow to feel isolated."

"So, Flow has a gambling habit?"

"Yeah, and again, I wanted to give them their money. But I didn't want them to kill themselves while using it. That's when I learned what I learned."

Canelo nodded. "Thanks. Gives me a direction to go."

"No problem." He paused. "Now I--."

"You want to know where Onion is right? Because we were able to find you so easily years ago. You figure we could do the same with Onion."

"Yeah."

"Well Arabia was a part of that. Why didn't you ask her to help you find him?"

"She won't."

"Maybe she's trying to protect you."

"I don't need her to protect me. I need her to hand this nigga over."

"The thing is, I gave Row my word that I wouldn't get involved. To try to prevent the Wolves and Vamps from clashing."

Cage was annoyed. "Why would you give him the word on something like that? I thought we were supposed to be looking out for one another."

"Because he doesn't want a war with the Vamps."

"I'm sick of everybody treating me like I'm an afterthought. I'm the only one that you need to be concerned about right now."

"True enough. But Onion is a troublemaker. And troublemakers make the loudest noise."

"He killed Magnus."

Now he had his attention.

"At first, he made me believe I did. But on my wedding day, as a fake ass gift, he told me the truth." He said sarcastically. "Tino didn't think I would pull the trigger. He was right. So, he sent him instead. He actually came through the window and took his life, Canelo. I can't have him roaming the streets at night. I need him brought to me."

Canelo was so angry his nostrils flared. "Give me two days."

"Fair enough."

CHAPTER FIFTEEN
"Tell me what you smell."

Cage and the Stryker Collection stood in an empty movie theater. Angelina was on his mind, as he woke up another night without her being in the bed but there was no time to ponder.

His collection needed his leadership.

The theater was beautiful.

Complete with red velvet walls and golden light fixtures, it was the type of establishment fit to play a Hollywood classic.

But this wasn't about watching a film.

Cage needed this space for one purpose and one purpose only.

And as always Arabia was by his side doing more observing than helping.

He turned toward her. "Do me a favor and bounce."

She laughed.

"I'm serious. Get out."

"Oh...okay."

When she was gone he said, "I brought you all here today because it's time to get clear on what I need from you." He took a deep breath. "I want to ask a question. Right now, what do you smell?"

The Vampires looked at one another confused.

"Is there something we should be smelling in particular?" Helena asked, eager to do a good job.

"Close your eyes. All of you. And tell me what you smell."

Within seconds, they yelled out things like new carpet.

Popcorn.

And even candy.

In the end they didn't give him anywhere near what he was seeking.

Disappointed, he said, "There will come a time in the not-so-distant future when we will have to defend one another. And that time may not be as easy to identify as someone standing in front of you holding a weapon. You'll need to be smarter. You'll need to develop and then use your senses."

They nodded.

"When that time comes, we must be able to think one step ahead of predators. And we do that by heightening our senses." He approached them slowly. "Come closer."

They did.

He raised his hand and suddenly the lights went out.

"Now tell me what you smell?"

The theater was pitch black and only the sounds of breathing could be heard.

Again, they yelled...Popcorn...Candy...Hair lotion.

Cage was getting irritated, but he remembered the compassion shown to him, when he was learning the new skill set for himself. And now that each of them had his fluid in their bodies he owed them a bit more patience.

"I don't want you to think of common smells. Think of the smell that makes no sense that you detect. Don't push that uncommon odor out of your mind because you don't see how it connects with this movie theater. Inhale. Be silent. And tell me what you smell."

"Yes, sir." A few of them said.

"Again, what do you detect?"

Silence.

"Don't let your mind go to anything else but the smell."

Five minutes passed.

Ten.

And then fifteen.

Nothing.

Cage could feel their anxiousness and annoyance. Even he felt irritated but if he was eventually going to get to a leader's headspace, he had to remain calm.

"Rain." Elena said softly. "For some reason I smell rain."

Cage smiled.

For the next fifteen minutes they practiced heightening their senses. Using the entire theater, in complete darkness, they tried to detect how close each other were based on the temperature changing in the room.

Cage wasn't just preparing for an attack.

He was getting miles ahead of everybody in The Collective as a whole.

When they were done Cage turned on the lights.

"This is the beginning. Practice more when you are alone. In the future you'll be able to smell different Vampires from other Vampires. No other collection has developed this skill. But you aren't like others."

"Sir, I understand the need to detect scents, but why should we develop the skill of detecting our own?"

"I pray The Collective as a whole will grow united. But we haven't reached there yet. And so, this skill will allow you to smell Vampires from afar, and our own too." He took a deep breath. "You are free to go."

They were so excited; most didn't go right away. Instead, they hung in the lobby area talking to one another.

As they busied themselves Cage attempted to make another call to his wife.

When her phone rang, and it went straight to voicemail he knew one of two things was happening. Either she was consumed with jealousy and actively trying to get back at him for The Fluid ceremony or she was harmed.

After he ended the call, Helena walked up to him. With his back still in her direction he inhaled the air. "Hello, Helena."

The scent of her lotion gave her away.

She smiled. "What you're teaching us, only Wolves know how to do."

"Not anymore." He turned to face her.

Damn she was pretty.

"What can I do for you?" He asked.

"Actually, I was coming over to see if I can do anything for you. You seemed out of it lately. And I just want to be, you know, whatever you need me to be."

Cage thought about his situation and even he was unclear of what to do at this time. Arabia was secretive about his general role. But he knew he needed to protect his collection.

"I just need you to focus on what we went through tonight. That's all I ask of you right now."

She stepped closer. "Yes, sir, I just want to be clear that whatever you need from me no matter how small or large I will do it. It doesn't need to be said and still I want you to know." Her fangs dropped. She covered her mouth. "I'm sorry."

Embarrassed that she was aroused, she ran away.

Just then, Angelina called.

By T. Styles

CHAPTER SIXTEEN
"Fall back, fall back!"

When Flow got out his car and entered the parking lot of a large warehouse, he could feel all eyes on him. Specifically, about fifty or so Vampires that seemed to hover around the front and sides of the building.

Sensing trouble, he stopped before attempting to make entry. The air smelled edible. "Is Onion inside?"

"And if he is?" One of the men asked. "Fuck you want with him, Wolf?"

Flow lowered his brow. "He's expecting me."

"That's funny because he ain't tell me shit about that."

As they moved closer, Flow's muscles popped, and he felt his body operating in a way he hadn't before. If it was fear that drove his chemical change, he was certain that he would be able to rip them to shreds before they knew what happened.

Luckily for everybody involved, Onion made his exit.

"Fall back, fall back!" Onion yelled to the O Collection.

"This how you treat guests?" Flow said, shaking his hand. "I was about to rip their fucking faces off."

They moved closer. "Try it then, nigga." One of O's members challenged.

"Everything is cool," Onion laughed, loving the show. "Right?" He asked Flow.

Silence.

Onion stepped closer. "Right, Wolf?"

"Yeah, whatever." He paused. "Who are they anyway?"

"Let's just say we're connected for life."

He patted him on the back and walked him into the building. The O Collection continued to look at Flow with a vengeance, until he disappeared inside.

"I'm here." Flow finally said when they were in private. "Let's talk."

"We'll get there. First let's catch up. Or are we gonna act like we didn't know each other in the past?"

"We knew *of* each other. There's a difference. Far as I can see now, you're different in every way. Had a facelift and everything."

"I didn't have a facelift."

"Then where are the scars? I still see a few but--"

"Does your brother know you're here?" Onion asked cutting him off.

"Why would you question me about that?"

"I just want to know how close you are to him these days. I mean, I know he got a new wife. Guess I'm trying to see if he's making her happy. Because if he's not, somebody else will."

"Put it this way, if you didn't see our birth certificates you wouldn't know we shared the same mother. Now what can you do for me?"

"My men and I do very well. The money flows with no problem."

"If there's no issue what the fuck do you want with a Wolf?"

"Let's put the thing out on the table. You and I both know that I'm Vamp. Which means I can't occupy the day like I explained to you already. But you can. So, I'll put you on to product. And you move it as you see fit. Bring back my percentage and we'll continue to do business this way for as long as we're getting money together."

"What are we pushing?"

"Roofies."

He nodded. "How much can I make in a week?"

Onion laughed. "The question is how much can you make in a day. We're talking thousands. Your life will never be the same after this shit."

"Since we're putting things out on the table let's talk about the main thing I want to know." Flow readjusted his step.

"I'm listening."

"Why you giving me this opportunity? Because at the end of the day you don't know me."

"I'm going to keep it clean. I don't fuck with your brother. And I know getting money with you will be the worst thing that could happen in his opinion."

Flow smiled. "I respect your answer. Let's get started."

As he continued to talk, little did he know that Canelo was sitting in position to see him enter the drug warehouse.

He didn't see who he was dealing with but he knew drugs were involved.

So, trust was damaged.

CHAPTER SEVENTEEN
"Cage prefers it that way."

When Angelina came home, she was surprised that all of the lights were out. Despite being pitch black, she was able to see figures moving in the darkness.

When she switched on the light, she saw ten members of the Stryker Collection in her home. Based on how they were walking around in pajama style clothing, it was obvious they were living there.

But it was Helena in her beauty that had her revving with anger.

"Why are the lights out?" Angelina snapped.

"Cage prefers it that way."

"Who are you?" Angelina asked, approaching her. "Really."

"You've seen me before."

"And still, I don't know you, bitch."

"First off, it's nice to officially meet you," Helena said with a smile.

Angelina didn't like her. After all, she had her husband's fluid in her veins. So that made her a direct threat.

"Who are you?" Angelina asked again. "Don't make me repeat myself again."

"My name is Helena." She extended her hand.

It was not accepted.

"I don't trust you."

Helena sighed. "That's unfortunate."

Angelina frowned. "Meaning."

"Because I have nothing but respect for you. You are my leader's wife. And since my only duty in life,

By T. Styles

which has been this way since I was a child, is to see him safe, then I want nothing but the best for you too."

"You also want my husband. I can see it in your eyes."

"You can say that after having one conversation with me?"

"I'm waiting for an answer, bitch."

"I'm not a liar, so I'll put it to you in the kindest way possible. Because truthfully, I don't think you could handle it any other way."

Angelina crossed her arms over her chest.

"I am here as well as the others to see to it that Cage Stryker remains safe and alive. And if it means dropping to my knees or getting on all fours to make him happy, then that's exactly what I will do. But understand this, I will never overstep those boundaries unless he desires."

Angelina was shivering, she was so angry.

"So, Mrs. Stryker, it seems to me there's only one thing that you should be thinking about during these times."

"And what's that?"

"How you can do everything in your power to keep him happy. So that I don't have to." With that Helena walked away.

When Angelina stormed through the bedroom, she saw complete darkness.

Flipping on the light switch she jumped when she spotted Cage sitting on the edge of the bed with his forearms on top of his knees.

"Why are you sitting in the dark? I don't understand what's going on in this house."

"I'm most comfortable in the darkness. Now where the fuck were you, Angelina?"

The lavender oil she had been accustomed to recently was overpowering.

Worried, she placed her purse on the table. "I didn't think you wanted me around. So, I decided to take a few days away from it all."

He stood up and walked slowly toward her. "Without telling me?"

Silence.

"You're a married woman, and yet you moving in the world like a bum bitch?"

"Excuse me?"

"You were gone for two fucking nights! And I was worried about you! I'm dealing with all this shit and you playing games with my mind? Do you want me to hurt you?"

She walked past him and sat at her vanity. "Cage, give me a break. You don't care where I am. You have your collection now and I'll be out of the picture before it's all said and done anyway."

His fangs dropped; he was so angry.

The scent of her blood had gotten so fruity, it smelled like synthetic candy.

"Do you want to be my wife or not?" He asked, pointing at the floor. "Because I need to know that shit right here and right now!"

"Why are you asking me that? So, you can get up with your precious Helena?"

"What you talking about?"

"She already told me that she's prepared to do whatever you need her to do. Why would you put somebody like that into your collection?"

Cage would deal with Helena later.

"Do you want to be my wife or not?"

Angelina took a deep breath and looked into his eyes. "There has been nothing more in the world I wanted than to be your wife. Just didn't expect it to be like this, Cage. To feel like this."

"And yet here we are." He sighed "What do you want, baby?" He held her hand. "Talk to me."

"Why didn't you offer me a position in your collection?"

"Because I don't want this for you! I don't want you only being able to see the moon and never witnessing the sun again. I want you to be happy."

"Well guess what, I'm not happy. I'm miserable. At least if you turned me then--"

He jumped up. "Do you remember the conversation we had on the boat that night?"

She walked away and flopped on the edge of the bed. "Yes."

"I made it clear that I would never convert you. So why are you asking me now?"

Silence.

"Angelina, fucking talk to me!" His fangs dropped.

"I just told you! And I'm asking because if you don't convert me, my fear is that our marriage will be over. And I don't want to lose you."

He wanted to show her compassion, but the mean streak they spoke about, the one that often happened the longer one lived as a Vampire, started to course through his veins.

"You smell sweeter these days. And it...it makes me want to hurt you."

"Why?"

"Because it means you're doing something you know is wrong."

A tear rolled down her cheek.

"They say the feeling I have is Vamp Rage. And I'm trying...I'm trying so hard not to...not to..."

"Not to what, Cage?"

"Kill you." He stormed out.

By T. Styles

CHAPTER EIGHTEEN
"We all stand on that."

Flow didn't know if anyone would come when he asked fifteen members of the pack to join him in the park that night, but he was serious about fattening his pockets and so he put out the word anyway.

Afterwards he waited.

When he saw the Wolves approaching the scene, he grinned inside.

Maybe Row was right after all. They would follow him anywhere. Of course, Row didn't think he would use his power in such money hungry ways, but he was moving rogue.

Shaking several of their hands he said, "Glad you made it."

"More of us wanted to come. But you made specific selections." He shrugged. "You mentioned money. So, let's start."

"An opportunity to make some money has fallen into my lap. And I want to offer all of you the same chance."

"Anything."

"Even if it meant making paper with a Vampire?"

They all looked at one another and back at Flow. "Before you came, the older packs wanted to outlaw drug money. And they definitely wanted us to avoid Vampires. But your brother is a bloodsucker. And if you think it's okay, me and my pack will follow you." He looked back at the Wolves. "We all stand on that."

Helena was shocked when she was asked to meet Cage alone in his Lounge. She figured she made an impression, but she didn't expect a personal invitation.

"Do you drink wine?" He asked as he sat deeper into his seat.

"Do you have anything red?" It was an attempt at a joke.

She hoped it landed.

It didn't.

He nodded toward the bar. "Go help yourself."

When she drank the liquid, slowly he rose and approached her. Judging by the rage on his face she moved backwards until she dropped in a seat.

"You finished?" He asked.

"Yes, master." She swallowed the lump in her throat.

"Good, because let me make something clear, bitch. If you ever talk to my wife about anything without my approval, I will snap your neck."

"I'm sorry. I didn't mean to--"

"Did you FUCKING HEAR ME?"

"Yes, master. Anything you say."

Taking a deep breath, he walked back over to his chair. "Is Arabia still here?"

"Yes, master." She trembled. "I think so."

"Tell her to come see me."

She hustled out of the room and Arabia entered. When she saw his chest rising and falling, she knew he was becoming fully Vamp.

"Your rage is bubbling. I can tell."

"I thought you said you picked the best people for me." He said pointing at the floor.

"I did."

"Then tell me why the fuck I had to reprimand Helena for talking to my wife behind my back?"

She frowned. "I don't understand."

"Apparently, she told Angelina that she would be willing to do anything sexually for me that I asked. Even if I wanted some shit like that, why would she tell her?"

Arabia shook her head softly and shrugged. "I'm sorry, where is the problem? Because I'm confused."

He glared. "What do you mean where's the problem? She's making shit worse in my marriage! May even be the reason Angelina stopped coming home. If that's the case I--"

"I assure you Helena is not the reason your wife is not coming home."

"Tread lightly."

"You still don't understand how the Collection works do you, Cage? When I tell you that they will lay down their lives for you, I meant their bodies too. So, when Helena talks to Angelina and gives her information that she's probably requesting anyway, she may not have been able to handle it. But it doesn't mean it's not true."

"I don't want her talking to my wife! About shit!"

"Then teach her! Teach them all! They are only as good as you make them."

Cage shook his head. The power that he now owned was weighing and he was concerned for many reasons.

Firstly, he was worried that if he wasn't careful, he would allow the power to go to his head. Blurring everything that he was trying to create and proving Magnus right.

And secondly, he was so attracted to Helena he was concerned that he would destroy his own home himself by fucking her in every room in that house.

"I'm finding it harder to be compassionate. How am I expected to lead anybody in this state?"

"You will either be like Tino or Magnus. You only have two choices."

PRESENT DAY
"The sun is overrated. I prefer the moon."

After a near bludgeoning, Violet was bruised more than she originally thought when she looked at her face in the bathroom mirror.

Blackened eyes.

Swollen lips.

Scratched neck.

Her greedy sisters, in an effort to rob her of her money, treated her like a stranger on the street.

In the end, she gave them the funds in her bank account, leaving her broke until her grandmother's next monthly payment.

Still, they had plans to come back for that too.

Had the beatings come from anyone else she may not have believed the vile things they said to her. But she knew when it came to cash, they would be willing to do anything to get a piece.

Which included beating her down emotionally and physically.

Walking to her living room, she flopped on the sofa. Every area of her body hurt. She was even too sore to get the pain medicine from her cabinet.

Just when she got situated, her doorbell rang.

She shivered.

Was it them returning to finish her off?

Slowly she rose from the couch and walked toward the door and looked out the peephole. Who she saw on the other side brought a sense of relief and fear at the same time.

After he saw her face, would he still think she was beautiful?

Opening the door, she said, "What are you doing here?"

He looked like he wanted to kill everyone walking when he saw her condition. "What happened to you my, Sweet Violet?"

"It doesn't matter."

She walked away and he followed her inside.

"I can't talk about it." She lie back on the couch.

"I won't leave here until you do." He stared at her with great concern and confusion.

"Please stop, Pierre. You don't have to pretend to care. You don't even know me."

"It's true. We haven't gotten the chance to spend much time together. But I will tell you this, I am the type of man who is in the business of getting an answer. Now what happened to you? Don't make me ask again."

"I was beaten."

"I see that. But why?"

"You wouldn't understand."

"Try me."

"My sisters learned that I'm the sole heir of my grandmother's fortune. And to put it simply, they don't like it."

"I'm still confused on why you're injured."

"They beat me and then they took my money."

"And these are blood relatives?"

"Yes."

Pierre took a long look at her and then he walked away.

"Where are you going?" She yelled.

He didn't answer.

162

Instead, he disappeared into her home as if he owned the place.

She could have followed him. Demanded that he leave.

After all this was her house. But she enjoyed his presence so much she would allow him to violate her privacy if it meant he would stay.

But Pierre exceeded her expectations.

Because what he did next, made her want him even more.

Twenty minutes later, she was the recipient of some warm chicken soup and crackers she stored for occasions like this.

Sitting next to her he carefully gave her the meal. "Eat. You need your strength."

Holding the bowl carefully, slowly she took the spoon to mouth while looking at his handsome face. Even her ex-boyfriend didn't care to help her heal when she had gotten ill in the past.

And here was a complete stranger, who did all he could to see to it that she was nurtured.

So, she drank every drop of the soup and when she was done, he carefully pulled her into his arms.

Awwww...this was the life.

He smelled of expensive cologne.

He smelled like money.

He smelled like power.

"I see myself in you." He said.

She looked up at him. "You do?"

"I was this way in the past. When I was a child. And I can tell you this my, Sweet Violet, it is unacceptable not to defend yourself. You have a right to be safe. And you have a right to maintain your own property."

"I'm not a fighter."

"That's something we're going to have to remedy."

She began to cry.

It was a hard cry.

The type of cry that made her believe that she had been holding back all her life and was finally given permission to release. Weirdly enough, in that moment, she learned with him she could be vulnerable.

The moment, in her opinion, was storybook.

And it made her want him even more.

When she was done shedding her tears, he picked her up and carefully took her to the bathroom where he ran a warm lavender scented bubble bath. First, he disrobed her and when she was naked, lifted her up and placed her carefully in the tub.

The strength it took to do so with ease gave her chills.

Once comfortable, he took the washcloth, dipped it into the water and allowed the suds and fizz to comfort her body.

From her face to her feet, he was careful not to miss an inch. She felt like he was a character that popped right out of a novel.

A novel that perhaps now that he was in her presence, she was willing to write.

In a sense Pierre had become her *muse*.

After she was clean, Pierre dried her off and placed her in the bed. Once she was situated, he removed his shoes, his pants and shirt before lying next to her.

Face to face, he looked into her eyes.

"I wish you could stay until the sun comes up." She sighed.

"The sun is overrated. I prefer the moon."

By T. Styles

She giggled.

"Are you comfortable, my Sweet Violet?"

"You have no idea." She grinned.

"Good. Because now I need something from you."

"Anything." She said, hoping he would finally ravish her pain ridden body.

"I need for you to tell me your sister's names. Now."

CHAPTER NINETEEN
"Just friends."

Blindfolded of course, Onion brought Angelina back to his house. This time he planned a storybook night that took her breath away.

Every tree in his yard was covered with white lights. In the middle of the lawn sat pavement over the grass where a single table was set up for two.

And damn did she look perfect for the occasion.

Wearing a tight black dress that exposed her cleavage, she allowed her hair to frame her breasts.

Onion wasn't a slouch by far.

Wearing a nylon t-shirt that had a slight sheen, he dressed it up with a pair of designer jeans. Because he wanted the night to be memorable, he saw to it that his hair was freshly cut.

No detail went overlooked.

Together with a bottle of rich designer cologne, he ate.

The moment she saw the magical set up her heartbeat increased. "Onion...this is beautiful. But it's too much. I don't want to give you the wrong--."

"Just friends. Let me do this for you. You deserve it."

She took a deep breath.

She was low-key tired of worrying about what Cage wanted when it was obvious he didn't give a fuck about her. So tonight, short of fucking him, she decided to go with the flow.

And she wasn't talking about the boy Wolf.

Sitting across from one another, under the stars, he said, "I had the chef make your favorites."

On God, everything she loved was on the gold rimmed plates before her eyes.

Blackened salmon.

Buttered rice.

Garlic with lemon asparagus and her favorite dessert.

Tiramisu.

Without any conversation about Cage, they enjoyed one another. They talked about the past and their lives together before Cage was even a factor. And she was taken back to when it was all about them. His friendship and love was solid, something she couldn't say about her husband.

Shit was going good and as the soft music acted as a backdrop for the evening, she got serious.

"Would you ever convert me?"

His original stance was to get angry. But rage ran her off before and he didn't want rage to run her off again.

"These hours I spent with you; are the best hours I've had in a long time. And still, it's not enough. No matter how perfect shit is, I only have you for twelve hours every day. I wouldn't wish this for you. So, the answer would be no. And I'm gonna have to demand that you not ask me again. If you love me, you wouldn't put me in this predicament."

She sighed deeply.

"You changed." She smiled. "I like it."

"Didn't change. Just realizing what I had when you were mine and dealing with it finally being gone."

Her pussy fluttered.

His dick hardened and his fangs dropped.

"I can't have sex with you."

He rose. "I know."

Standing before her, he lowered his height so that he was on his knees. Pulling her chair to the left and right, he raised her dress. To breathe in her flesh, his nose pressed against her thighs.

She wanted him so badly her clit vibrated.

"What...what are you doing?" She breathed heavily.

"I just want to taste you." His tongue ran over his fangs, and she was so turned on she was about to scream.

Removing her panties, his moist tongue found her tunnel. Taking the trip, he ran it in and out of her pussy.

"Damn, girl. Why you so fucking wet?"

"I...I can't fuck you."

"It's not about that. I promise I won't touch you that way until you beg me. Just...just let me taste your sweetness. Please."

The gel coming from her pussy sent him on fire. Slowly easing his tongue to the top of her clit, his tongue flicked back and forth.

And when she felt his fang glide over her button gently, her entire body lit on fire. If he wanted he could've eaten her alive, and she would have enjoyed it, knowing he would love every bite.

Onion flipped, licked, and sucked her so well, she grabbed the back of his head and pressed into his face. This was the type of grind that if she weren't careful, she could take a Vamp's life due to suffocation.

But the shit felt so fucking good.

When she was about to cum, he lifted her up. And while her pussy was still in his face, he drank every drop like fresh water from a glass.

"Onion...oh my...oh my, gawd!" It was the hardest cum of her life and she felt weak for wanting more.

Why did it have to end so soon?

When he put her down, her pussy brushed over his dick on the way to the ground.

But she was determined not to go there.

To her, the pussy, although wet, still belonged to Cage.

Instead, she dropped to her knees, found his staff, and placed his stiffness between the plushness of her lips. She was using the same ideology she had as a teenager. That as long as she didn't have sex, there was no crime.

With one hand on her shoulder, his head dropped back as his dick pulsated and moved in and out of her throat. She was a professional, so she did the chore without a gag.

He wanted her since she left him, so it didn't take him long to explode in her mouth.

Now it was she who was drinking from his body.

When she was done, she stood up and looked into his eyes.

"I love you, Angelina. And I need you to know that it ain't about nothing else with me. But please, I'm begging you, come back home."

CHAPTER TWENTY
"You said he was the answer."

Cage was gonna kill that bitch.

For the past couple of nights when he woke up, she wasn't at his side. He was on the brink of insanity.

Driving his car, he headed down the road to meet someone with information he had been waiting on for a very long time.

If Onion had her, if he touched her, or made love to her...

The thoughts were too evil.

He would pluck his limbs out one by one and pop her eyeballs out with a spoon.

He needed to get his wits about himself, or he would lose complete control.

Standing outside of a hole in the wall restaurant, Canelo approached him.

"Where's Onion?" Cage asked, breathing heavily.

"You're not going to say hello first?" He folded his arms over his chest.

Silence.

"I haven't been able to find Onion. I'm sorry, man."

This shit was getting on Cage's nerves.

Had he had the sun he would've solved the case a long time ago.

"So, you had me come all the way out here for nothing? This nigga had the police come to my house and everything."

"Hold up, I was able to get in touch with Berg, Pigsty and Langley like you suggested. Together we were able to locate most of the members of his collection. That's why I wanted to meet."

"So, he did convert?" Cage scratched his head.

"Yeah, I figured you'd know already."

Now this was getting good.

"How many?"

"Not sure, but I have an idea that it's about fifty."

"That means he knows how many I converted too."

Could be true. "Not sure how he could've found out though, but we believe he converted about a week ago."

It didn't matter.

There was nothing that was going to stop him from getting what he wanted.

Him on his knees, in front of him, begging for his life.

"How many were you able to find?"

"I was able to validate about fifteen. If you follow them I'm sure at some point it will lead to Onion or his right-hand man Cheddar."

It wasn't what he wanted to hear, but it was a start. Shaking his hand he said, "Thanks, Canelo. I have it from here."

"Before you go there's something else I want to talk to you about."

Cage nodded. "I'm listening."

"It's about Flow."

"Isn't it always?" He shrugged.

"Actually, this is bad."

"How bad can it be? He already doesn't listen. He been reckless!"

"He's getting into the drug business. And bringing some Wolves with him."

Cage was furious.

Fuck is wrong with this nigga? He thought.

"You and your brothers asked for him in the library. I gave him to you. Because you said he was the answer."

"I know but--"

"But what? I leave him with you and now he's a drug dealer?"

Canelo's muscles popped.

Cage's fangs dropped.

If things didn't get civilized within seconds, shit would get bloody instead.

"I understand why you're upset," Canelo whispered. "But you can't forget that we're not some dumb ass niggas off the street. He's our nephew and we want the best for him. And because he's your brother, we know you want the same."

"Are you sure about this information?"

"Positive. He's been followed. And we're concerned."

"I need to think about my next moves. He's at the age where he doesn't want to listen so it's hard controlling him." In a sense, Flow reminded Cage of himself when he was getting on Magnus' nerves.

"We will do what we can too." Canelo promised. "But he's arrogant. And that trait is hard to work with."

"I won't let him hurt himself. If I gotta do what I gotta do, then so be it."

"What does that mean?" Canelo frowned.

Silence.

"Cage, Flow's greatest concern is that he believes you killed my brother. So, if you come clean and tell him you didn't maybe he will--"

"Don't get him involved!" He pointed in his face. "I want him to stay out of this."

"Why?"

"I told you already! Because I believe he will approach Onion. One of the reasons I want Onion found is to prevent that shit from happening. So, Onion is *my* problem, not his."

"When are you going to let up off that money then?"

"Let me handle my brother and his finances. We'll leave it at that, Wolf." Cage got into his car and pulled off.

CHAPTER TWENTY-ONE
"I'm trying to protect you."

Flow was driving down the street at a quick pace. The weather was comfortable, but he was sweating because of what was on his agenda.

First, he needed to hit it to Onion's warehouse and then get up with Mink. It would be the first time he would talk about sex with a female and so he was mostly nervous.

He was about three miles away from Onion when his phone rang. He hit the car speaker. The moment he heard Cage's voice his muscles popped. "What you want?"

"That's how you talk to your brother, lil nigga?"

He sat back and dragged a free hand down his face. "You're not afraid of me no more? Because you looked shook in the car the last time I saw you." He laughed.

"The only fear I had was what I was prepared to do to you if you didn't calm the fuck down."

"Are you calling to give me my money? Or are you calling me to tell me you figured out a way to bring dad back to life?"

Cage sighed. "I'll spend the rest of my days trying to make what happened to pops right. That doesn't change the fact that you're my brother. And we have to get along."

"There's nothing you can do for me. Except give me my paper." He turned the corner. "Like I said, are you calling to do that or nah?"

"I already told you you'll get the money when the time is right. Now ain't it. I even let you see the account of your finances. All the levels are in order."

"I saw it. I see you put a little guilt money in it too. But the thing is, until it's in my pocket, it doesn't really exist now does it."

"I'm trying to protect you."

"Big bro, the last time I needed you to protect me, I was in that bitch's basement with my siblings, being treated worse than a dog. So, I don't need you to protect me anymore."

"You out of line, Flow. But I'll take your hate as long as you're safe." He paused. "In the meanwhile, I think we need to spend more time together."

He laughed. "Again, not interested."

"Okay let's do it like this, I want you to know that whenever you need me, I'm here. I don't care what the topic is about."

Originally Flow wasn't trying to hear shit he was saying.

In fact, he was about to hang up. But then he remembered he needed to know about the birds and the bees.

At the end of the day, he was clueless about what would happen once he had sex with Mink.

Could he trust his big brother?

Flow bit his tongue several times before finally deciding to come clean. "There's something I want to talk to you about. I mean...I really don't need your help but--."

"I'm listening."

"Why did you kill my father, nigga?" He said before hanging up.

He chickened out.

Fuck him. He thought to himself.

He would never trust him again and as far as he was concerned, he was dead.

He will learn the birds and the bees by fucking instead.

Pulling up in front of Onion's warehouse he was greeted by several of Onion's collection members. When he saw his men suddenly aim weapons over his head, turning around he was shocked to see they were pointing at Bloom instead.

What was she doing there?

The O Collection was about to gun down his sister before his very eyes.

"Hold up!" Flow yelled with outstretched arms. "That's my sister!"

"Then why the fuck is she creeping around?"

"It's not like that!"

Suddenly Flow found his muscles popping again. And when he looked at Bloom, he could see her body swelling slightly in her clothing too. It was obvious that they were ready to attack.

Shit was going to get bloody.

"Put down your weapons!" Flow warned.

Just then, Onion walked outside and when he saw Flow, with Bloom he smiled.

He always took his fucking time.

"You mean to tell me I get to have two Stryker siblings in my possession at once?" Onion said, rubbing his hands together.

Flow wasn't feeling the comment, but he would leave it alone for now.

Turning around he asked her, "What you doing here? Why are you following me? Did Cage send you?"

176   By T. Styles

"No, but I overheard from Canelo that you selling drugs. And I think he told Cage."

Flow was heated. But that explained the call from his brother.

"Did he tell him who I was working with?"

"I don't think so. But what are you doing? This is fucking crazy!"

"If they didn't send you why did you come?"

"Because you're my brother. And I wanted to make sure everything was okay. We don't talk anymore."

"I'ma be honest, now is not the fucking time."

"What you gonna do, Flow?" Onion asked, interrupting. "I don't have all day like I'm sure you know already."

"I'ma walk my sister to the car."

"It's cool. Come inside." He looked at Bloom. "Both of you."

Flow sighed and walked inside with his sister.

While he and Onion talked business in the basement of the warehouse, Bloom stood in the far corner next to the door out of earshot.

She stared at Onion's fine ass from afar.

"Why you let her in here?" Flow asked. "I just found out my uncles know I'm pumping."

He glared. "They know you working with me?"

"No. But I don't need her causing problems."

"I asked her to come in because I want to talk to her about a few things. The last time she saw me, we got off on a bad foot. And I want to see if things can be different."

Flow wasn't feeling it one bit. "Whatever you and I got going on, leave my sister out of it."

"Like I said, it's perfectly innocent. I'm not putting her into anything. Just want to clear the air." He placed a heavy hand on his shoulder.

Flow shook it off.

"Let's not worry about all that right now." Onion continued. "The package we talked about has been delivered. It's segmented and everything. Divvy it out amongst the Wolves and then bring me my percentage."

"And then what?"

"If shit goes smooth, you'll get another package later."

"Is that it?"

"Yeah."

Flow shook his head. "Make whatever you got to say to my sister quick. I'll be waiting outside for her."

"I'm only going to talk to her for a few minutes." He placed his hands together in prayer. "You have my word."

Flow walked toward Bloom and said, "He wants to rap to you. But the countdown for five minutes has begun."

Since Bloom had been attracted to Onion from the beginning, even after he almost attempted to come into the gate and take them away when she lived with her aunt, she was eager to smile up in his face.

First, she had some questions.

"What are you doing with my brother?" She crossed her arms over her chest.

"Now you know I can't tell you that. But what I want to know is what took you so long to find me?"

She knew everything about him was dark and yet there was something about him that she still found irresistibly attractive.

He moved closer.

178　　　　By T. Styles

And he smelled so fucking edible.

"I'm just here to let you know I have my eyes on you."

"Is that right?" He grinned.

Arrogant in nature, Onion leaned in for a kiss. What better way to get back at Cage than to get his little brother hemmed up in the streets, win Angelina back and fuck his little sister?

Despite being virtual strangers, she allowed their lips to meet.

At first the kiss went about without a hitch, and then her stomach growled.

She couldn't control her urges.

She couldn't control her flesh.

Before she knew it, she bit down on his bottom lip, causing a piece of skin to dangle.

Wanting to eat his flesh, she kissed him again quickly and pulled the meat from his mouth.

He shoved her backwards. "Fuck is wrong with you?" He yelled, his fangs dropping.

"I...I don't know..." She chewed the meat, and it was so edible, it caused her pussy to tingle.

Placing his fingertips against his lips he looked at his own blood. He would heal later but that shit hurt *now*. "Are you crazy?"

"I don't know why I did that." She cried. "I...I don't know."

"Get the fuck out of here!"

"Onion, I'm--"

"Now!"

What brought her fear in that moment was not that she bit him, but that after tasting his flesh, she wanted another bite.

Just one small nibble.

And she vowed to do it again.

By T. Styles

CHAPTER TWENTY-TWO
"I need the Vampire they call Onion."

It had been a long day as Cage worked with his collection even more on developing their senses. As time went by it became obvious that they would die for him, and if shit kicked off he may have to hold them to their word.

Under the moonlight, they developed their sense of sight.

They even perfected their sense of smell so well that the Stryker Collection could detect one Vamp from another.

More than that, they could sniff out Onion if he was within twenty feet of their king.

And they did it all within darkness.

When they were done working Cage brought them together for a private conversation.

They were in the living room of his home drinking fresh blood, which he kept their bellies full on. This was different from some leaders who demanded that their members hunt for them instead.

Cage was generous in that way. And no one questioned how he obtained such a massive supply.

They didn't give a fuck.

They were fed.

They were satisfied.

And they were strong.

When he glanced around at his beautiful people, his eyes rested on Helena, who per usual kept stock of every word.

Every glance.

"There is something I want to share with you all."

Cage's chest was bare, with nothing but his muscles percolating under the *Magnus* chain, if truth be told a few of the female Vamps wanted to fuck him in that moment. While the men wished to be one percent of who he was becoming.

"Although some may not understand how what I'm about to ask is necessary for the survival of our future, I ask anyway."

"Anything you want you got." Langley said.

They cheered in agreement.

Cage nodded and sank deeper in his seat.

"There is a nigga out there, who's still breathing, who caused problems for me and my family in the past. He killed my father. And I got reason to believe he may be playing a hand in dismantling my family now. No, scratch that, he possibly fucking my wife."

They gasped, knowing of the Wolf who raised him and the woman who shared his bed.

"And while I take some responsibility for bringing him into our lives, I need him to meet his end."

They moved in closer, careful not to miss a word.

"What will you have us do?" Helena's eyes showed she was ready for war.

"I need the Vampire they call Onion to feel my pain. And thankfully, with Langley and a few rogues, we were able to locate members of his collection. So, if I can't have him, I want you to weaken the walls that keep him protected instead. I want you to kill each member of his collection. And I will show you how."

They looked at one another.

Although it wasn't said, it was obvious that this was serious. To hunt another master's collection meant that in time a target could also be placed on their heads.

And at the same time, if Cage had beef on the streets, they took that shit personally. Because if he died, each member of his collection would experience pain like they couldn't imagine.

"All I need is an address," Eric said, cracking his knuckles. "And you can consider it done."

Cage appreciated the way he got to the bottom of shit.

"Langley, give them the details."

Langley rose. "We have about fifteen names and their locations. If shit goes as planned, they should be unearthed and killed within a week."

"King, we got you on that shit," Helena said to Cage. "But I want you to have total satisfaction." Her words were deeper, and Cage caught her meaning. "Do you know where the one who killed your father and is bedding your wife rests his head?"

Cage sighed and drank every remnant of the blood.

"Onion's smart and conniving. Was that way when we were kids. To make matters worse, he spent time with my blood father. It won't be easy. So, I'll say this, if you see him, bring him to me. If you can't, because it's not safe, kill him instead."

"How?"

Cage slowly got out of his chair and raised the chest that held the wooden stake. Opening the lid, he removed the dagger and raised it high. "It's old school but it still works. This through the heart should do the trick."

All nodded in agreement.

When they were about to settle down Cage walked up to Helena. Grabbing her hand, he pulled her away from the rest.

"I smell a scent on your skin." He stared into her eyes. "I know what it is."

She stepped back and he pulled her closer.

"Don't move."

"I'm sorry." She shivered. "I just wanted you to...to have what you wanted."

"I smell Angelina's lavender all on you."

"I wasn't near her when...how can you even do that? She had to be at least fifty to one hundred feet away."

"What did you find out?"

Helena swallowed the lump in her throat. "I followed her one night to see where she was going. I was close enough that I could've touched her if you desired. Instead, I waited."

He stepped closer.

No room between them.

"What did you see?"

"She was at a restaurant with a Vampire. I know he was a Vampire because I smelled rain. Hard rain."

Cage trembled with rage. "And his face?"

"Faint scars."

It was Onion.

"And what else?" His breathing increased.

"He blindfolded her and then I think he spotted me. Because he drove fast. And I lost him."

"Can you show me the place?"

"Of course."

Later on, that night Cage went to the abandoned restaurant where Angelina and Onion first met as teenagers. He was so angry he felt as if he were floating.

184   By T. Styles

If this was what she wanted, then so be it.
But he had plans too.

Cage was preparing to talk to Arabia about Angelina when his sister knocked on his bedroom door. He had roughly six hours before he would get tired due to the sun taking to the skies.

And at the same time he would always make time for Bloom.

"Sister, are you good?" Cage asked.

She looked worried. And in her eyes he saw a fear he had never seen before. "Can I talk to you about something?" He patted the bed next to him.

"Come here."

She shook her head slowly. "No."

He frowned. "Why not?"

"I don't want to hurt you."

Enough said.

"Go on," he responded.

"I was around someone a few days ago. And he stepped in front of me. When he did, I felt an attraction towards him that I never had before." She touched her gut. "It...it felt like hunger but sexual."

Cage rose. "Go ahead."

"And I'm afraid of this feeling." A tear rolled down her cheek. "I'm afraid I won't be able to stop it."

"When you said you felt an attraction and hunger, I need you to go deeper."

To be clear he understood what it meant to lust and have a hunger for a person. By all accounts he was a Vampire. And Vampires always lusted for blood and sex preferably at the same time.

Yet his fear was born from the knowledge that at some point in time, Wolves would crave their flesh.

He needed to see if she was already awakened.

"I want to have him near, brother. So I can...so I can have him. So I can consume him."

"This person, who was he?"

She looked down. "I can't tell you that."

He stepped closer, despite his life being in danger. "You see, that's not going to be good enough. I need you to tell me now."

"I won't do that, brother. And it's not because I don't trust you. I'm afraid of how you would look at me. I just need to know is there anything I can do about it?"

With little to no information he decided to keep his words simple. "If you control your urges, you can control your flesh."

Tears rolled out of her. "But what if I can't? Because as I stand in front of you, I have that same attraction now."

By T. Styles

PRESENT DAY
"If you feel that way, how can it be selfish?"

Chloe was sitting on her knees, in front of a shampoo chair with the owner of the salon wearing nothing from her waist down. The salon owner's husband, Wayne, was to Chloe's right and he was looking intensely at the duo.

Despite being female, Mrs. Salon was one of Chloe's most profitable clients. Because every week at the same time she would invite Chloe to her shop to show her husband how to eat her pussy.

It wasn't that he didn't do an okay job.

He definitely did what was necessary for her to reach an orgasm.

It was just that he hated eating pussy so much that the chore had become to show him how to fake it as opposed to showing him how to do it.

And since Mrs. Salon owner had made it painfully clear that if he didn't satisfy her in all the right ways in the bedroom, that their marriage would be over, he gave this his undivided attention.

Chloe took her hand and spread the left and right pussy lip apart. Next, she gave the middle a light squeeze, which caused the clit to peak out and glisten under her touch.

With a tongue as wet as the Nile, she lapped up, down and side to side while she suckled softly. Mrs. Salon was so in awe of her pussy game that she moaned as if she were crying. Although the Husband wasn't with the gay shit, he did have to admit that even he was turned on.

Within two minutes, Mrs. Salon exploded in her mouth.

"That was fucking amazing, Chloe," she said.

"No problem." Chloe rose, wiped her mouth, and looked at Husband. "You ready to finish her off?"

He nodded and assumed the position.

"I got it from here."

After getting paid her two grand, Chloe stomped to her car to make it to the bank before it closed. Although she spent a little more time than she wanted to at the shop, she prayed the bank would still be open so she could make a withdrawal.

It wasn't.

"Damn!" She said to herself. "I got to start making them keep the time they pay for without going over."

Since the bank was closed, the ATM would have to do.

Although she couldn't make the amount of withdrawal due to the limit, she decided to grab half of the money she needed to put a down payment on a new apartment.

She smiled when she checked her balance and saw it was just as it should have been. After all, her sister, Violet, after they beat her down, gave her five grand to show mercy from the beat down.

And the plan was to do this each time she saw her face.

Hustling back to her car after making a light withdrawal she was surprised to see her tires were flat. The beauty salon owner's shop was in a newly developed area and so there was gravel and construction equipment everywhere.

She figured she got a flat tire due to rolling over a nail but didn't understand why all four were down.

Taking her phone out of her purse to call for help, suddenly a chocolate man in the Mercedes Maybach pulled up beside her. He was so fine her jaw dropped.

"Are you okay?" He looked at her tires. "Looks like you faced a little trouble."

"That depends."

He grinned. "On what exactly?"

"Well, if I say I'm okay and you pull off I'll be disappointed. But if I say I'm not okay and you help get my tires fixed and then pull off later, I'll still be disappointed. So, what we gonna do?"

"I got a few ideas."

"I'm listening."

"I say we get your car towed somewhere safe."

"I like where you're going but I want a little more," Chloe said, applying slut on extra thick.

"And then we can go somewhere where I can help alleviate the disappointment you feel."

"I think my tires getting slashed was the best thing that happened to me all day."

"So, your day was worse than this before?" He leaned back in his seat.

"You wouldn't believe it."

"I'm listening."

"I just finished up with a client but a little while ago I learned that my grandmother who is wealthy doesn't care about me as much as she does others."

"What gave you that impression?"

"I don't want to sound selfish."

"If you feel the way you feel, how can it be selfish?"

"I'm not the best granddaughter in the world. But I still care about my grandmother. And I want the best for her. But it's not always perceived that way. Because she has a favorite."

"You're telling me an awful lot at this moment. I guess I should feel special, but I know there is another reason," he said.

"There is. It's because I want you to know my side of the story."

"Your side of the story?"

"I know who you are." She glared.

He smiled. "Word?"

"I know you're seeing my sister. I remember seeing your face outside when you dropped her off. Different car. Same man. Must got a lot of money." She crossed her arms over her chest "So my question is, what the fuck do you want from me?"

He laughed once. "You may want to start by telling me who your sister is."

"Her name is Violet. But you know that already."

"Ohhh yeah." He snapped at the air. "Violet is an acquaintance. Right now, you are an acquaintance too. If you don't want to accept my invitation, don't. I'll just leave you to it. So, what do you want to do?"

"Don't get it twisted. I don't care if you're fucking my sister. I'ma still go anyway."

"So why are you wasting my fucking time?"

CHAPTER TWENTY-THREE
"Life for me is different."

Tatum was in his room on social media. It didn't matter if he spoke in front of the camera or if he danced or cooked meals his audience held on to his every word. He was considering some new content when Cage entered.

"Hey little, bro. You good?"

"That's weird." Tatum got up from his chair and flopped on the side of the bed.

"Because I'm asking you if you good?"

"Yeah. Because usually when you wake up you want Angelina to do your thing and then you check on us for--"

"I get it," Cage laughed, embarrassed that he was referring to him fucking his wife. "But right now, I'm seriously asking how you're doing."

"If you mean do I like living here the answer is yes. And I don't wanna go."

"That's something for me to think about because you are the only person I'm a hundred percent sure is ready to be on their own."

"I get Flow, but you don't feel that way about Bloom?" He frowned.

Cage realized that due to her awakening, having her near was dangerous. And letting her go on her own was worse. "Not right now."

"What's going on, Cage? You freaking me out."

"I need you to do me a favor."

"Okay."

"I need you to follow Angelina in the sunlight."

He frowned. "Why?"

"Because she's been keeping time in the morning with something or someone and I don't like it. And I need to know where mine is at all times."

"Won't she get freaked out if I follow her?"

"Not if you don't tell her."

"I don't know about this."

Cage walked deeper inside. "Life for me is different."

"You're telling me. You're a Vamp and I'm a Wolf."

"I'm not talking about that."

"I was just playing."

"I know you are. And if I had more time I could joke around too. But that's not the case. Every hour I'm awake is valuable. And I'm concerned that my wife may be up to something. I would go to Shane and Ellis, but after Savannah grabbed them, they've done for me what they could and now they need the time to reconnect with their families."

"I'll do it."

"If it was going to be that easy, why you give me such a hard time?" He laughed.

"Because, I don't know, having her around felt like the old days." Tatum shrugged.

"I don't get it."

"Angelina cooks for us. Helps us with anything we need, and I can tell she really wants to do a good job for you."

"A good job?"

"Yeah. She's working at some office."

This was new. "Wait, Angelina has a job?"

"You didn't know?"

"Nah." He paused. "Besides, we got money. And she has access to her own funds I set up. So, there's no need for any of it."

He figured she was telling him a lie.

But why?

"She mentioned that, well, she wasn't sure if you still wanted her to be your wife."

"Why would she say some terrible shit like that?"

Cage knew why.

Because she was possibly fucking Onion.

And he would kill her too.

"I don't know. But when she thinks me and Bloom ain't looking, she cries a lot."

Cage was annoyed.

The fact that she was showing cracks in their marriage drove him up a wall. "Shit ain't been perfect with us. But my wife doesn't have to have a job unless she wants. So, none of this shit makes sense to me. Did she tell you where she works?"

"No. She doesn't talk to us a lot about details. The only reason that came out was because we run into her on her way out sometimes."

Cage dragged a hand down his face. "I need you to follow her and find out where this job is."

"If I do this, I don't want her knowing I was involved." Tatum said. "And I don't want you to hurt her."

He sure hoped he wouldn't make him promise.

"She's that important to you?"

"Like I said, she's cool. That's it."

"Okay, it's done." Cage nodded. "Did you see her this morning?"

"Yeah...I see her every morning. But I think she makes it her business to be gone when you wake up. And I don't know why."

CHAPTER TWENTY-FOUR
"That's the future. Wolves and Vamps getting along."

The club was jumping.

And Onion and Flow were getting closer as the days went by and they continued to accumulate wealth with one another.

Sitting in VIP discussing their recent business ventures over blood for Onion and liquor for Flow, the two were in worlds of their own.

Glancing at his drink, Flow asked, "What does it taste like?"

Onion took another sip. "If I tell you, you still wouldn't understand."

"That's why I'm asking for clarity."

"You like your liquor, right? And you prefer weed with a drink like a mixer."

"Sometimes." He shrugged. "But sometimes I like it straight up."

"Well blood is like mixing your strongest liquor, with your best pill, while getting your dick sucked. Then make it times two."

"That's how I feel when I eat flesh." Flow said.

"What kind?"

"Any kind to be honest. I just want to taste the--"

"Blood." Onion said finishing his sentence.

Flow reasoned that maybe they had more in common than they both realized.

"Bloom, is she okay?" Onion asked, remembering the bite to the lip.

"Why, did you do something to my sister?"

"If I did, do you think I would be asking?"

By T. Styles

"Then why bring her up?" Flow shrugged.

Onion wanted to mention the lip biting, but he wasn't sure if she was being freaky or trying to kill him. "No reason." He paused. "So, tell me why you fell out with your brother."

Flow didn't feel like his high getting broken, but the constant questions were annoying. "Do we have to talk about this shit?"

"It's the one thing we have in common, remember?"

"He killed our father."

"How do you know?"

"He all but admitted it."

Onion sat back in his chair. After all he knew Cage didn't murder his father because he had. What he didn't understand was why he didn't tell him.

Cage was holding info for a reason and Onion wanted to know why.

"So, but for the murder of your father, you and he would still be close?"

"Of course. What else other than betrayal can separate a family?"

"I could think of a few things."

"Not me." Flow drowned all his liquor and waved the waitress over for another.

"It's a shame you can't get closure." Onion persisted.

"I used to think about that all the time. Making amends with my brother. But now that it plays on my mind maybe it's not natural for Vamps and Wolves to get along."

"You saying that to the Vamp who employed you." He allowed his fangs to drop *just 'cause.*

"We're business partners. Business relationships always break barriers."

"I don't know about all that. I think Vamps and Wolves can get along especially if the relationship is mutually beneficial."

"I just want to stack enough money to do a few things I have in mind."

"You mean outside of gambling?"

Flow glared his way. "I play the horses, so what?"

"It's not my business either which way."

He continued as he looked out into the club where Werewolves and Vamps were mingling amongst each other. It was amazing how both races were able to coexist in full sight of the Norms.

"What you do is your prerogative." Onion laughed once.

"So why bring it up now?"

"I've seen plenty of people being brought down based on waging worthless bets."

"Already got a brother. Had a father. Don't need that from you."

"Like you said, we are partners. Which means I have a vested interest in you." He pointed at him. "It's also important for you to know that I don't bite my tongue. I bite necks instead."

Flow didn't say it, but he liked his answer because he knew where he was coming from.

"What I do on the side won't bother you. If I give you my word then you have it. As long as you don't change, things will remain the same."

"I guess we'll see."

As they continued to converse, across the way a female Wolf and a male Vampire held a sexually explosive conversation. On the surface they looked unassuming.

By T. Styles

But an attraction was brewing.

"You see that over there?" Onion said to Flow proudly.

Flow peeped it a while ago. "I saw it earlier."

"That's the future. Wolves and Vamps getting along."

The beginning of the war had begun.

CHAPTER TWENTY-FIVE
"I made a mistake when I made you my wife."

When Cage woke up he was surprised to see that Angelina was next to him. Slowly he rose and dragged her out of bed by her hair.

"Get off of me!" She yelled, slapping at his hand.

He released her to the floor only when he was good and ready. "Where the fuck have you been?"

She sat on the edge of the bed and looked at her reflection in the mirror. "I needed my space."

He wanted to smack the shit out of her, but he had to bring his rage under control. "Angelina..." he took a deep breath. "Cut the fucking games. Were you...were you..."

He needed to ask if she'd been seeing Onion.

But his pride was getting in the way. Surely she wanted him from the gate. So that meant Onion could never be a problem, right?

She turned to look at him, almost as if begging with her eyes for him to be a little jealous. To do something to let on that he really cared.

"Were you with the nigga Onion?"

That wasn't what she was looking for. "Did you really have...did you really have Tatum follow me?"

Damn.

Little Bro fucked up the assignment.

"I thought you didn't care, Cage. I thought you wanted me gone so that you can have your space. Why do that?"

He grabbed his robe. "I never said that." He slipped it on.

"That's how you treat me! I'm starting to despise you."

"If you hate me so much why do you fuck me when I'm asleep?"

"I haven't touched you in weeks. Haven't been interested   either."

Her words were like wooden daggers to his heart. Was she getting the dick from Onion instead?

"Angelina, for your own good, you need to leave this house." He whispered.

"Cage, you are so mean when you want to be. Which lately is all the time." Tears rolled down her cheek.

"Did you hear me or not?"

"I love having sex with you. If I could do it every day all day I would. But that's not our reality is it? Which leaves me taking it as I can get it. So yes, I fucked you a few times when you were out."

"If I find out that you were seeing him, you'll see my darkest side."

"So, you're threatening me now?"

"A threat is only a threat when the person receiving it feels guilty. And you fucking Onion, or even being around him is treason in my eyes."

"This is so hurtful."

"I'm still waiting on a response."

"I don't know how to answer that. What I am saying is that I'm no longer willing to sit by and be used like a toy. It's all or nothing, Cage! Do you know what that means?"

"Get out." He pointed over her head.

"Excuse me?"

"I'm not playing games with you anymore. I made a mistake when I asked you to be my wife."

She placed a warm hand over her heart. "You would do that to me even though you swore to protect me?"

"You want it both ways. And that's not how I'm moving. I got a lot of troubles already. I don't need more from a fake ass wife too."

"I don't want to leave."

"Based on how you're moving, I don't know if that's an option for me anymore. Because for real, I don't trust you. And I don't trust myself around you."

Losing him was going too far. "Okay, was I trying to get attention? Yes. Maybe I did too much. But my heart was in the right place."

"Why you still here?"

"Because there are so many things going on in my mind right now. And I need you to hear me out, Cage. We may be arguing, but at least we're talking, which hasn't happened in a long time."

"You? All you have to worry about is what makeup you wanna wear to stop time from showing on your face! My troubles go deeper."

Her eyes widened.

Hearing him attack her aging beauty hit differently.

"I never thought you would say something like that to my face."

He wanted to apologize. Truly he did.

But Vamp Rage took over once again.

"You heard me. Our troubles aren't the same. You have two weeks to get out. That should be enough. Either way, I don't give a fuck."

CHAPTER TWENTY-SIX
"Did you taste it or not?"

The young Vampire and the young Wolf walked into a motel room together. After meeting at the club where Flow and Onion conducted business, the moment they laid eyes on one another, the attraction was instant.

With that type of chemistry, they had to go somewhere a bit more private.

Rue, the young Wolf, stood in the middle of the room and admired Leigh, the young Vamp's beauty.

Dragging her berry scented locs over her shoulder, she smiled at him. "Why are you so perfect?"

Sitting next to the lamp on the counter, his beauty sparkled under the golden light. "I could say it's genetic. But you know that's not true. Don't you?" He paused. "Anyway, being attractive is all subjective. Because everything about you...your body, your face, I find just right."

Young Wolves were built like athletes.

While Vamps were fit but possessed far more physical attributes one would consider easy on the eyes.

"Now, we came here for a reason." He rose and readjusted his growing dick. "And I wanna see what's good."

"Do you crave my blood?"

"Nah...but I crave that Wolf pussy."

She grinned. "Why?"

He shrugged. "Cause it's different."

"I've never had sex with anybody before."

He frowned. "For real? You a virgin?"

"Yeah." She blushed.

"Well, I guess I gotta be easy with it then. Because I don't want to hurt you."

He was cute.

But only a male Wolf's dick could hurt a female Wolf's pussy.

"You know why I invited you here?" Rue said with all the confidence in the world.

"I got ideas."

"It's clear that Wolves and Vamps aren't supposed to get along." She stated.

"Who made that rule?" He asked.

"I don't know. But is it true?"

He moved closer, away from the light and into the darkness.

"Well Vamps don't subscribe to rules. And I don't make decisions based on other people either. I make them based on me and what I'm feeling. And what I'm feeling right now is you. So, what's on your mind?"

She smiled. "If I tell you I crave you and that I long to taste you, would you fear me? Because it's true. And so, I ask, what greater love is there than that?"

"So, you love me now?"

Silence.

"You smell so good," she continued. "I want to see what's good with that dick too." She gripped it softly.

"Oh, so you not playing no games, huh?"

"You said you wanted to be serious so here it is." She laughed. "Besides, ever since I saw you in the club I couldn't help but breathe you in."

"I never heard that before. To be *breathed in.*"

"You're about to experience things you never experienced before too." Now it was Rue who moved closer.

"Tell me more."

"All I could imagine is being next to you and tasting you."

He was stiffening in his jeans. "Is that right?"

She stared at him harder. "Yes."

Shoving him to the bed, she crawled on top of him. She was a Wolf, so she moved in a predatory nature. But he loved every minute of it. Because lately Wolves appeared to exalt Vampires and so Vamps considered them exotic.

In a sense, he was dating out of his race.

When she placed her nose at the center of his neck she inhaled deeply. His dick hardened so much, it hurt.

He needed to relieve himself within the walls of her pussy or else.

This wasn't a blood thing.

He didn't want to taste her.

Because to Vamps, Wolves smelled of wet dirt. Despite this, because they were closely connected to nature, they were still very appealing.

Within seconds they were both naked and he was almost ready to bust that back out.

But then something went wrong.

Immediately she lowered her head again and bit into the flesh of his neck. The moment she tore into him, her body was stimulated with many erotic sensations.

Like electric pulses.

But instead of it stimulating one part of her body, as she satisfied her hunger, her pussy got wet too.

"What are you doing?" He yelled as he shoved her across the room with his Vampire strength.

Rue jumped back on the bed with the quickness of a cheetah.

Leigh tried to fight her off and did a good job. His strength wasn't normal, and so he had much of it. The thing was, each time she jumped on him, and bit his flesh, she weakened him.

Back and forth they went, with blood painting the walls.

But in the end, he succumbed to her power. Because instead of blows, she took to nipping at his body.

Why was this happening? He thought.

When he was done, half breathing and on the verge of death, she flopped on the edge of the bed and called the women in her pack for help.

"What have I done?"

Vamps could heal, but they needed time away when they were destroyed. And it didn't look like it was going to happen.

She had gone too far so as if she were in a sleep, she had finally awoken.

They arrived, ready to assist. The plan was for them to provide a way out.

Instead, the moment they smelled his flesh, they wanted more. And so, they lowered their height and ate at him too.

When they were done, there was barely anything but bones.

All of them had awakened.

Full and sexually stimulated, they took to pleasuring themselves around the room.

It wasn't until each of them reached separate orgasms, that Rue, ashamed and confused, ran to

204   By T. Styles

the phone to make the most important call of her life. She would reach out to Magnus' son. The one they said understood the youth.

"Flow, I need your help."

"What happened?"

"Please come," she cried. "It's important."

Twenty minutes later he arrived to see what the women in his pack were capable of if left to their own vices.

This wasn't a killing.

This was a massacre.

But when he smelled the scent of the Vamp's blood, he understood why. So, slowly he walked over to a small bit of flesh remaining and took a bite.

The odor was erotic.

After having a taste, he would never be the same. He was certain.

What was this feeling?

Racked with guilt, he backed away.

Not knowing what to do, or why he had such dark thoughts, he called his uncles Row, Shannon, and Canelo for answers.

Not that it mattered much now, but this violent moment meant the war between the Wolves and Vampires had officially begun.

The uncles stood in front of their nephew, in a park, enraged.

"What's happening?" Flow asked with heavy breath.

"Nigga, you the one who killed a Vampire!" Canelo yelled. "You tell us!"

"I don't...I don't know." He walked away and returned. "By the time I got there the girls had taken most of him. But the smell of his flesh...it...it fucking attacked me."

Row walked away with his hands on his hips. "There is a lot that you don't know. But what I want to know is this, did you taste the flesh?"

Silence.

"Flow, did you taste it or not?" Row yelled.

He nodded yes.

"Then you aren't safe around Vamps ever again. Even your brother."

Flow's eyes widened. "This is why my father wanted Cage gone. He...he craved his flesh too. Didn't he?"

They looked at one another.

"Row, Canelo, Shannon, please tell me honestly, did my father eat...did he ever taste Vamp flesh before?"

"Yes." Row said, looking down.

"And now you have to let us know every move you make. Because you will crave them too."

CHAPTER TWENTY-SEVEN
"Be careful, Helena."

C age sat in his bedroom, alone with the lights out. When he finally realized what his life was being shaped into, he decided to embrace it.

Originally he wanted to be married, because truth be told there was no one more important to him than Angelina.

This was still true.

But she had proven herself to be weak and weakness was not what he was willing to put up with any longer. And still he knew he needed her to be safe before they separated officially.

There was a soft knock at the door.

He took a deep breath. "It's open."

Helena walked inside. Her face was as pretty as the petal on a blooming rose. "Do you need me?"

He frowned. "What do you mean?"

"You taught us senses, and to pay attention to everything around us. Well, I discovered that if I try, I can feel when you need me the most. And I feel you need me now. Am I wrong?"

"Come inside."

She entered.

"In the future, I need you to give me space, while I figure out what's going on with my wife."

"I will never disrespect you, king. I adore you too much. But I'm still waiting on an answer. Do you need me or not? Because if you say the words, it's whatever."

His dick jumped.

"I don't necessarily need you. What I want you to do is what I ask. Isn't that what you signed up for?"

"When you reprimanded me because of my actions against your wife I accepted that fully. Besides, I knew there was nothing I could do. You were right. And I was wrong. But look at you now, Cage."

He loved the sound of his name on her lips.

"You are a king. And you don't even know it because you have chosen a woman who doesn't understand our struggles. She's so angry she isn't able to consume every minute of your day, when an hour is more precious than all the diamonds in the world." She placed a hand over her heart. "To me."

"I know who I am."

"Do you?"

"Be careful, Helena. Or you will soon find out."

Slowly she moved toward the bed. "Why do I still feel you calling me to you, even though you say otherwise?"

She was right.

"Can I touch you?" She begged.

Instead of saying the words, he used his mind to say yes. He wanted to see if it worked.

It did.

And so, she crawled on top of him.

Removing her shirt, she allowed her long hair to frame her breasts. His fangs dropped, hers did too.

And he found it sexy as fuck.

She was a reflection of himself.

A better version of everything he liked about being a Vampire.

Removing himself from his boxers, he entered her pussy in a way he never could with Angelina. They were made for each other, and it showed. When the

By T. Styles

dick rocked to the left, electric pulses shot through his body. When it moved to the right, the same.

With every pump it was as if he was exploring areas no man had ever gone before.

Using his mind he asked, *"The night of the ceremony, was I your first?"*

"Yes," she said. *"I was waiting on you to choose me."*

He was stunned, not knowing this power was available to him.

"Don't worry, you can control what we know. You control everything, Cage. So, I can never read your mind if you don't want me to."

He fucked her hardcore.

There were no mentions of love. Feelings or emotions. Just pussy to dick, and he was hooked.

She was too.

Bloom took Cage's advice to connect with her own, and so was in the recreation center for Wolves.

Instead of the packs mingling just with their own, they commingled, and so she found security in that place. Especially since she developed a taste for Vamps that she was concerned about.

She was about to leave when she heard Rue and two other Wolves talking about tasting Vamp flesh.

"I...I don't know what will happen." Rue whispered.

"Did Flow seem mad when he showed up to the motel?"

Now Bloom was definitely interested since her brother's name came up.

"Yes. He seemed confused too. But...but I want to do it again," Rue whispered. "I feel like I'm supposed to do it again."

"Me too," another said.

They all looked at one another. "But we can't tell Flow. Or the Elders."

Bloom didn't know their plans, but whatever they were, she wanted in.

Walking over to them, they quickly looked down. After all, she was Wolf royalty being Magnus' daughter.

"So, you're hunting Vamps?" She asked.

Silence.

"Answer me!"

Rue cleared her throat. "Please don't tell."

"I won't. Because next time you're taking me with you."

Cage sat in his lounge thinking about the night before with Helena.

They said the right woman on your arm added power to the cause of a man. The thing is, which cause did Helena aid?

By T. Styles

He hadn't planned on cheating on Angelina, but with that one interaction alone, he learned that the power of his collection extended in ways that most collections were probably unaware of.

They could read each other's minds.

This was a game changer.

Sitting by the phone, he waited for Langley to call him with details. Finally, it rang.

"What happened? I've been waiting all night."

"Sorry, sir."

"What happened?" He said firmer.

"We found everybody on the list. The fifteen."

He smiled. "Did you follow my plan? To refrain from killing them until they led you to other members of Onion's collection."

"We followed it to a T."

Cage sat back in bed.

He was pleased.

"We now know where forty-nine live, sir."

"Forty-nine? Who's missing?"

"We don't know."

He nodded. "Go on."

"We know where they frequent. We know the women they prefer. What will you have us do now?"

Cage had to be careful.

And at the same time, it wasn't like it was rocket science. For him to be king and bring his people to whatever end necessary for mankind, he needed Onion gone first. Which meant he needed his collection annihilated.

"Use the D viles I gave you to poison their blood if you can. If that doesn't work, use the stakes."

"Yes, sir."

With his mind Cage said, *"Leave no one alive."*

"*Done.*" Langley heard him.
Cage grinned.

By T. Styles

CHAPTER TWENTY-EIGHT
"You can't trust new niggas."

Bloom, Rue and two others followed one of the members of Onion's collection. He had just gotten out of the warehouse. From afar, they tailed his car and when he parked, they eased out of Rue's truck.

Had he developed his senses, he would've smelled the attack coming.

He didn't.

Besides, Onion didn't make developing senses a requirement to be in his collection. He didn't even know that was an option.

And so, the young Vamp was prey.

The young Vamp approached his fence when Rue stepped up and said, "Hey you?"

The moment he laid eyes on her; his dick took over. "Damn, you fine."

She whipped the locs over the side of her shoulder and said, "For real?"

"Yeah, what's your name?" He asked.

"Whatever you want it to be." She snapped and Bloom and the other two girls came out. "You want to join me and my friends for a party?"

"Fuck yeah!" He said opening the gate.

Ten minutes later, he was eaten alive.

Onion was sitting on the edge of his bed when Cheddar walked into the room.

"What the fuck is happening?" Onion looked out, confused. "I...I don't understand how in less than two days, I had two members of my collection be eaten alive."

"We don't always get the answers the way we want. Sometimes shit pops off for a bigger picture."

Onion chuckled once. "I just had two members of my collection be eaten alive. Why is that possible? What is going on with the Wolves? Because I'm not gonna let this go unanswered. I hope you understand this."

"Do you really want me to say it?" Cheddar crossed his arms over his chest.

Onion looked at him. "I asked a question didn't I?"

Cheddar, realizing he was pushing his limits, took a deep breath. "You should not have trusted the boy Wolf."

"You mean the grown man?"

"You know what I mean. Although some believe that at some point we can merge, at the end of the day we're different species. And different species can't always get along." He sighed. "But I came here for another reason. A worse reason."

"What is it now?"

"Forty-seven members of your fifty are dead. Cage put out the hit."

By T. Styles

Onion rose slowly. "I felt it in my heart."

"You're under attack, Onion. And right now, Cage is winning."

"Forty-seven? Who got away?"

"Looks like the girl Carmen escaped."

Onion felt like he wasn't angry enough. "I lost forty-seven members and you don't have anything else to say? How can they be of any service to me if they're dead?"

"I want to be honest with you. You need to break ties with the boy and Angelina."

"I'm done with him. With her I can't...I mean I won't let her go."

Cheddar sighed. "When Tino finally decided to take his seat at the head of the table for The Collective I was drained. When he died, I said I would never help another leader ever again. And yet here I am assisting you."

Onion was waiting for him to say something he gave a fuck about.

"I will give you the same advice I gave him. Advice that he never took to heart. Advice that would've saved him. From you."

Onion glared.

"You can't trust new niggas."

"I disagree."

"You let someone into the camp. You exposed yourself. You thought it was enough for money to roll in to appease people who may have felt disadvantaged because of you. But you underestimated what Cage felt the moment he found out you killed his father."

"What can I do now?"

"We can start with breaking your connection with Angelina. And cutting ties with Flow." He paused. "And then we have to go over both of our heads."

"Meaning?"

"There were some things that Tino and the Elders knew. Things that they refused to tell us. And while I'm sure everything done in the dark comes to the light, we may have to help them niggas along."

"Are you saying take out the Elders?"

"I'm saying we should do whatever we have to, to get answers. Because at the end of the day, they know something. Which is why they got ghost the moment Tino died."

"I also underestimated Cage." Onion admitted.

"At least now you know. Now it's time to do something about it."

"You're right. But I'm not giving up Angelina. So don't ask me again. She is the deal breaker."

CHAPTER TWENTY-NINE
"Threats are instantly perceived by the guilty."

Bloom and Rue were at Cage's house, in Bloom's room.

After tasting the second Vampire, they were fiening for their next feast. Standing in front of each other, they played over and over what happened and how eventually the party they were about to experience was over because Onion's Vamps were gone.

"How do you know?" Rue asked.

"I overheard my brother talking," Bloom said. "All of Onion's men are dead. I can't believe all that good food is gone to waste."

Rue walked away and plopped on the edge of the bed. "Then what we gonna do now? Cause I can't...I can't stop." When Helena walked past Bloom's door, Rue looked at Bloom. "You think he would know, if we...if we...took her?"

Bloom closed the door and walked over to her. "I don't know. Should we?"

"Maybe we should try." She whispered, excited about the possibilities.

Five minutes later while Helena was in the lounge getting blood from the fridge, the girls cornered her.

"What do you want?" Helena asked, frowning.

"Cage is on the phone in my room." Bloom said.

She lowered her eyebrows and removed her cell phone from her pocket. "Why hasn't he called me?"

"I don't know."

"Well, where's your phone?"

"Like I said, it's in my bedroom."

Helena glared. "If Cage wants me, he can reach me without the use of a phone."

"Why are you acting scared?" Rue giggled. "We just want you to come with us."

"I don't know what's going on, but I want you both the fuck up out of my face." She stepped closer. "Am I clear?"

They looked at one another, smiled and walked away.

Lying in bed, Mink looked at Flow with concern in her eyes.

"You've been quiet, Flow, what's up with you? And why are your uncles clocking your every move?"

He looked at her. "Something happened, and, and I don't know what it means for the Wolves and the Vampires."

She frowned. "The Vampires? Why do we care about them?"

He couldn't tell her about the cravings.

Something in his heart said it was too soon. It was mostly shame.

"I can't right now."

She took a deep breath. "Well, what we talked about, the other thing, I think I'm ready now."

By T. Styles

Lately she didn't want to talk about sex, so this was new.

His eyes widened. "I thought you said you weren't sure because--."

"I know what I said." She laid on her back. "But for a female, choosing a Wolf is final."

"I don't understand."

Nobody ever told him.

"Since our bodies aren't open until we have sex, selections are serious for women. Because once I do this, my pussy will forever be built for you. And nobody will...nobody will want me."

Now it made sense.

"I'm not leaving you, Mink. I promise."

"I'm trusting you, Flow." A single tear fell from her eyes, and he was shocked. Mink was hard bodied, and so he knew emotion didn't run a dime a dozen for her.

"I'm not going nowhere. You can count on me."

She nodded. "Okay, let's go."

After laying a towel under her body, first he kissed her forehead. Next, he kissed her cheeks. Her neck and her breasts. He wanted to take his time, because the first time for a female Wolf was as painful as taking a bat to the pussy.

But once the skin was broken, the pleasure was twenty times better than it was between two Norms.

When the towel was laid, he moved toward her. Stroking himself to a thickness when he was hardened the length was 18 inches.

The width was eight inches.

This shit was a monster.

He was so hard now, if he wanted to turn back he couldn't and so she widened her legs.

This was happening no matter what at this point.

First, he pressed softly against the tiny hole, which broke the skin.

Raising her chin due to the pain, Flow slowly continued while kissing her face softly, trying his best to appease her. Tears rolled down her cheeks as he went deeper and deeper and blood dampened the towel under their flesh.

There was no stopping now.

"I'm not leaving you, baby," he said in her ear as her body quivered in pain. "I swear I'm not going anywhere."

Wrapping her arms around his body, she cried into the pit of his shoulder as he continued to push deeper. As mounds of blood poured out of her, suddenly he reached the furthest level within her box.

The moment he tapped that center, the pain went away, and she moaned in ecstasy.

He raised up and looked at her face. "I'm there?"

She smiled and wiped the tears away. "Yes. It...it feels so good."

Now it was time to have fun.

He hugged her and eased in and out of her, as the blood was now replaced with a gel-like substance. She was in so much pleasure now, her legs wrapped around him as she pulled him closer into her body.

She wanted more.

The pussy was definitely Flow's at this point.

Mink hadn't realized that tonight would be the most pleasurable and painful moment in her life.

When they were done, as they lay in bed his mind wandered again. "What you thinking about now?"

She had given of her body. So, in his opinion, she deserved honesty.

220   By T. Styles

"Rue ate one of Onion's men."

She rose up. "So...so it's true?"

"You heard about it?" He frowned.

"Yeah, but I thought they were rumors."

"Nah, bae. They ate a Vampire to death. Had him spread out on the floor like a deer caught in the wild."

"Were they starved?"

"Fuck no. And then when I told my uncles, they didn't seem shocked." It's like...like..."

"Like what?"

"Like we're drawn to Vampire flesh."

"What about you?" She asked, afraid about the future.

Silence.

"What about you, Flow? Do you crave it too?"

"When I first walked into the room I was more embarrassed than anything else. I couldn't believe the pack had gone so far. But when I smelled the flesh lying on the floor, I got it."

"What I hear you saying is that you don't know if it's one and done. Have you spoken to your partner? Onion?"

"Nah."

"I think you should."

"And if he doesn't want to talk to me?"

"Then fuck it. Because he'll regret the day he ever sent you away."

Flow called Onion at about 9pm that night. The phone rang once, and he answered immediately.

Sitting in his lounge, Onion said, "Fuck you want with me, nigga?"

"Listen, I don't know what happened the other night but--."

"What happened is that your people ate my folks. Fuck is up with that?"

"Can you hear me out?"

"Are you calling me with questions or answers?"

"I'm not calling with either."

"Then I repeat, what the fuck do you want?"

"I'm saying maybe you and I should talk and hash things out."

"What I know is this...in less than 72 hours two Vampires in my collection were eaten."

"Two?" Flow said. "I didn't know nothing about that shit."

"Yeah, whatever, nigga. Understand this, when I get my come back ready, no Wolf is safe on these streets. And that includes you and your people."

"Why that sound like a threat?"

Onion hung up.

Cage had just finished speaking to his collection when Helena stepped up to him.

When he saw Bloom and her friend walk by, she grabbed his hand and said, "Can we speak the Vamp way?"

Since Cage wanted to make sure his thoughts were protected, he thought about something irrelevant at first.

"Are you talking?" She asked. "Because I can't hear you."

It worked.

He used his mind again, but this time directed his thoughts toward her. Now she heard every word.

"What is it?"

"Bloom and her friend were going to attack me."

Cage frowned. *"What do you mean?"*

"I feel like they wanted to do me harm. Like they were both attracted to me and wanted to hurt me at the same time. And I think we should be careful."

As they continued to talk with their minds, Bloom and her friend Rue looked at them from a distance.

He immediately knew she was right.

It was 8 am when Rue opened Cage's bedroom door. She had stayed the night and decided to look in on the king.

Standing in his doorway, she breathed in his flesh.

"What are you doing?" Bloom asked, walking up behind her.

"Onion is going to kill him," Rue whispered, as if he could be awakened. "What if we put him out of his misery earlier."

Before Rue knew what happened, Bloom's body bubbled and using her strength she clawed at her face.

In fear, Rue fell to the floor and held her face while looking up at her.

"Don't look at me, bitch," Bloom said.

She readjusted her gaze to the floor. "I'm sorry."

"You are no longer allowed to come to my house." She said breathing heavily. "Get out! Now!"

Rue jumped up and ran away with no shoes.

Breathing hard, Bloom looked at her brother once more as he slept. She also used to come to the room to smell his sweet flesh. She told him it was because she wanted to make sure he was still there.

She mostly lied.

And as she looked at his sleeping body, she said to herself, "What's happening to me? I don't want to hurt you. Please."

CHAPTER THIRTY
"At the first sign of trouble you dump me?"

Cage was celebrating! He successfully took out most members of Onion's collection. Although he was sure he weakened him, he knew it wasn't a true success. In the end, he attacked a bunch of Vampires, too sloppy and careless to put up a good fight.

And as a result, they chased pussy and blood.

A deadly combination.

To be fair, that didn't take away from what his collection accomplished.

By practicing the art of their senses, they calculated the exact moves to attack.

They were the better collection.

And so they survived.

It was far from over.

They needed to be smart because as they spoke, Cage believed in his heart that Onion was planning his revenge.

Standing in the ceremony room, Cage said, "I'm proud of each and every one of you tonight." He raised a glass filled with imported blood. "I could not have done any of this without you. But it would be unfair of me to give off the notion that we are done."

Most of them nodded their heads.

"He will definitely make a move. But his moves will be futile. And not backed with enough skill for what I'm planning next."

"So, it sounds to me like we have the better leader," Helena said.

The Stryker Collection went off in excitement.

He raised his hand and calmed them down. "No doubt."

"Talk that shit, boss," Langley said.

"Settle down," Cage joked. "For now, if you're not on duty here, I want you to go home. Be with your significant others. Be with your families. And wait for my next orders."

None of them seemed excited about the break.

"Why aren't you leaving?"

"If it's all the same to you boss, I think it's best that we stay here and protect you." Eric said.

"You're the only family I give a fuck about," Langley said.

This was unity.

They were one.

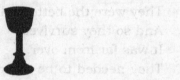

It was 10 am and Bloom was getting ready to hunt sleeping Vampires.

She was about to meet Rue to plan her attack, but when she opened the door Shane and Ellis were standing in the doorway.

"What are you doing in my room?" She asked.

They moved closer.

Unlike other Vampires, since they hadn't taken The Fluid, they didn't smell like fresh meat. Instead, their scent was giving two niggas who were there to snatch her ass away.

More than anything, they could walk in the day.

226

"Get out of here!" She yelled.

"Nah, little sis." Ellis said, grabbing her by the arms. "You coming with us."

Later on, that night, Ellis called Cage when he was awake. "She's in the storm shelter like you requested."

"Good."

"But you know how I feel about locking someone away. She's your little sister."

"I know. But if I had any other choice, I would take it. At the same time, my life was in danger. I smelled her and her friend when I woke up one night. Like they had been in my room. And I couldn't shake the sensation."

"I feel you. I'm not sure, but I got the sense that she was plotting something before we pulled her away."

He sighed. "See to it that she has everything she needs. When I'm ready, I'll go see her too."

"We got you."

The uncles looked at Flow with great disappointment as they stood in the backyard. "What's wrong with you, little nigga?" Row asked, stabbing one fist into the other. "I thought I told you eating Vamps was out!"

"I didn't have nothing to do with the second one! Or the first since we making a list!"

"Then who did?" Canelo yelled.

Suddenly Flow's muscles bubbled, and he was ready to attack. But when he saw Canelo, Row and Shannon do the same, he reverted back to a regular sized buffed ass little nigga.

They were the bigger wolves.

They were bound to beat his ass to a pup.

"You don't have to come at me like that."

"Oh, but I do." Canelo said. "Not only were you getting money with your brother's enemy but then you placed members of various packs in the mix. And quite possibly put us at war."

Flow didn't know they knew about Onion.

"I always thought it was you but now I'm starting to realize I was wrong." Row continued.

Flow was fucked up by the statement. His uncles hadn't always been in his life, but losing their respect hurt. "You thought it was me?"

"It's a fact that one of Magnus' sons is meant to take over the whole pack." Row said louder. "But you're selfish. And you're angry. So, it can't be you."

Flow walked away and came back.

Part of him knew that they were correct, but the other part hated how they felt as if they were better than him. In his opinion, had Cage given him his money he never would have had to resort to selling drugs.

But he didn't.

Which left him no choice.

"You know what, I'm tired of y'all coming at me any kind of way. I'm a grown man."

All of them growled lightly.

By T. Styles

"I'm doing y'all a favor by even being around any of you niggas," Flow continued. "You don't know what it's like having full knowledge that you're higher than any of your circumstances."

"Now who sounds like they think they're better?" Canelo responded.

"I don't think I'm better; I know I am. Remember? Magnus' blood pumps through my veins." He beat his chest as if someone gave a fuck.

Canelo smelled him. "Oh, you had some pussy and now you talking reckless?" He laughed.

He was surprised that they knew that too.

"Yeah, we smell it on you," Canelo laughed. "You picked the meanest one in the pack. I hope she don't kill your ass."

"You can't stay here." Row interjected. "If you think you got things under control, go at it alone."

Flow glared. "Hold up, you're throwing me out?"

"Why should you care?" Canelo chuckled once. "Remember you got everything under control. You don't need nobody but yourself. So, we calling you on it."

Flow crossed his arms over his body. "I didn't mean it like that."

"It doesn't even matter at this point. Go make good with Cage. Talk to your brother. And see if he will allow you back into his good graces. Because we're done here."

The thought of having to grovel sent Flow on a new type of rage. But still, he didn't want to go.

He was a Wolf.

They were a part of his pack.

"Row, you gonna let them throw me out?"

Silence.

Row didn't even look at his face.

"You know what, I knew y'all niggas were fake. At the first sign of trouble, you dump me? Fuck every last one of you bitches."

"Go talk to your brother." Row said once more. "And get the fuck up out my house, pup."

They bopped away.

When they were out of ear distance Shannon said, "You know we can't abandon him."

Row nodded. "It's true. But we know why we need him. He needs to discover why he needs us too."

CHAPTER THIRTY-ONE
"Correction, I took out his collection."

Cage was entertaining his collection when he went to grab more blood from his lounge for his team.

After all, by taking out the O Collection they made it clear that they were serious business.

The power was real.

On the way to the living room, he was shocked to see Angelina walking inside the house.

"Just so you know I was in your bed when you woke up, but you looked at me and rolled back over."

"Yeah, I was exhausted. Had a long night the day before and I guess I needed more rest than I realized. The thing is though, I still want you gone."

"You gave me two weeks and I need every day."

"Whatever, man."

"But I want this marriage, Cage. And I know I've told you this before, but we really need to spend some time together speaking alone. Away from the collection and the airs you put on for them."

"Airs?"

"I know you, Cage. And you were nothing like this when we were kids."

"Of course not! I'm a grown man! And I'm a Vampire!"

"You know what I mean."

Sensing his distress, ten members of his collection entered. *"I'm fine,"* he said to them with his mind.

They nodded and walked away.

Focusing back on her he said, "The truth is, you didn't know anything about me. If you really had, you wouldn't try to change me now. And I'm telling you again that I know things."

"Things like what?"

"That you were with Onion. Blindfolded. And at his house."

She farted.

"Cage, can we talk?" Arabia asked, interrupting the two.

"How come every time I want to talk to you she pops up?" Angelina yelled.

Cage looked at Angelina and said, "At the end of the day it's like this, I want you out of my house in two weeks. I won't say it again."

Angelina shook her head and walked away.

"What's up Arabia?"

"I heard about what happened."

"I need more."

"You went after Onion's collection."

"Correction, I took out his collection."

"I told you to leave the revenge game alone. Why didn't you listen to me? Instead, you go against my word and now you've involved your own people in a battle where many will die. That's no king."

"You wanted me to be a king. I didn't ask for the shit."

"You're right. I thought you were capable. Now I realize you just trying on a crown that doesn't fit." She paused. "At the end of the day you're a lost cause."

"I'm sorry you feel that way."

For real he wasn't.

He just wanted her out of his face.

By T. Styles

"I need you to make me feel that I'm not wrong. Do you want to help The Collective and the Norms or not?"

"Why is that my job, to save these ungrateful ass Norms? Still, I was willing to do what you needed. All I asked was that Onion be dealt with. And you denied me."

"If you hurt him more damage will be done to your collection than you realize."

"Well at this point, it's whatever."

"Are you aware that several Wolves are already eating Vampires? The war has been triggered, simply because you chose to fight with your brother, Onion, who is also a fellow Vampire. And you know what, I'm done helping you. I'm done with all of this. Good luck."

When she attempted to walk away he snatched her arm and his fangs dropped.

He shoved her so hard against the wall, she peed a little.

"I could snatch off your face and take your life if I desired." He smiled. "Convince me not to."

"There's that evilness I knew was there. What are you going to do now, Kill me?"

Slowly he released her, and she stormed out.

Angelina had packed a bag and left Cage's Mansion.

Since he was too concerned with the trials of Vamp life, she realized she was done and didn't need the two weeks.

That didn't stop her heart from hurting.

She would rent herself an apartment and start all over from scratch.

Without Cage.

For the moment, she was done with Onion too after he grilled her for hours about Cage's whereabouts.

In the end she felt like a game between them both.

She was almost to her car when she saw Flow driving in the parking lot.

Slowly he exited his car and approached her. Looking at her bag he said, "Is everything okay?"

"You know what...I can't even call it, Flow." Tears rolled down her cheeks.

"Well, what happened?"

"I'm done with your brother. I'm done with his selfishness. All he seems to care about is revenge."

Flow stepped closer. "Revenge?"

"I don't have all the details. All I'm sure about is that being in this marriage is not something he's interested in anymore."

"Damn, shawty." He tucked a few strands of hair behind her ear. "I liked you for him."

"What are you doing here? I thought you lived with your uncles."

He sighed. "They threw me out. I'm basically here to see if Cage gonna let me chill here until I get a place of my own."

"If I were you I would go as far away from here as possible. His collection is so far up his ass you won't be able to find him."

"I'm not sure about that. Bloom and Tatum seem to like it here. Even though I haven't been able to get in contact with her for the last couple of days."

She took a deep breath. "Don't get me wrong, Cage can be caring when he wants. But when his mind is made up he's narcissistic and arrogant. All he wants right now is Onion's head."

Flow had a current situation with Onion, so he knew this was quite serious. "Let's do each other a favor."

She sniffled and wiped her eyes. "I'm listening."

"Eventually I'm going to have to go into this house and beg for mercy." He said playfully.

"You can still run." She smiled.

"No, I can't. Because at the end of the day I realize he's my brother. And my uncles turned their backs on me quicker than I thought they ever would."

"I understand."

"So how about we go grab something to eat. Come up with a plan on life for both of us. And then perhaps tomorrow will be better."

"I don't know. I'm not good company right now."

"Come on," he said playfully. "Do it for me. Besides, what do you have to lose?"

PRESENT DAY
"Let me put a smile on your face."

Jeanette was a complete wreck.

She and Chloe were so close that she didn't realize how devastated she would be after not hearing from her in two days. Although she had clients eager to pay her for her sexual services even that seems foolish at the moment.

Quite honestly all she wanted was her sister.

All she wanted was to make sure she was safe.

She was on her way to grab something to eat when she realized her card had a zero balance after trying to get some gas. This was shaping up to be the darkest moment of her life.

Figuring she would have to service a few clients after all to make a come up, she hit it back to her car when she saw someone leaning on the side.

Unlike Chloe she didn't recognize his handsome face.

"Is there any reason you're leaning on my car right now?"

"This was my way of getting your attention. Is it working?"

There was something about him that drew her immediately. "Actually, it did work but I'm not in the mood."

"Maybe I can help you with that."

"And why would you care?"

"Ordinarily I wouldn't but since I like what I see I'm hoping I can put a smile on your face. Will you give me an opportunity to do that?"

By T. Styles

Jeanette broke down crying, due to the kindness he was showing her.

He walked up on her and rubbed her back softly. His height and his confident touch made her putty in his hands.

"Okay so you're definitely going to have to tell me what's going on now. I can't leave you like this."

"My sister has been missing for days."

"Is she young? Because teenagers have a tendency to--"

"No, she's in her twenties. But this is unlike her. We're sisters but we're more like best friends and she would never go days without calling. And it's driving me crazy."

"Well, do you have any relatives? Mother? Or father?"

"My mother died some time back and I'm not sure where my father is. I do have another sister but she's so green and stupid that I would never go to see her anyway."

"But maybe she's with her right now."

"I know it's hard to believe that not all families get along, but I'm telling you she would never be caught dead at her house."

"Okay what can I do for you? To make your day a little bit better. And whatever it is, it doesn't matter."

"Short of bringing my sister back..."

"You know I can't do that since I don't know her location."

"Then I don't need anything else."

He stepped in front of her. "Are you sure? Because you could use a friend even though it may not help your current predicament."

"I don't know."

"Can I take you to get something to eat?"

"I mean..."

"Let me put a smile on your face. If after all of that you still aren't having a good time then you haven't lost anything have you?"

"I guess you're right."

"Do me a favor, pretty lady and say yes."

She smiled. "Yes."

By T. Styles

CHAPTER THIRTY-TWO
"You want to be queen."

The night air was cool and refreshing.

Flow was on his way to scoop up Mink to tell her about the night he had with Angelina, when suddenly he saw Shane and Ellis hovering in the shadows. He didn't recognize them, but he could tell it wouldn't be good.

"Aye, Flow, you gotta come with us right quick." Ellis said.

"Why I gotta do that?"

"Because your brother wants to holla at you for a minute." Shane smiled. "I mean you are still--."

Flow took off running but they caught him as all three hit the ground.

Holding him to the cool concrete, Flow's muscles suddenly swelled up and he pushed both of them off. Catching up with him again, they managed to hold him but suddenly Ellis was met with a four-prong scratch across his face.

When he looked down at his own blood, he noticed that Flow's fingernails were longer and his body had expanded so much, he was pushing the limits of his clothing.

This would be a fight they hadn't prepared for, but luckily Cage planned everything out in advance.

"When you meet him he'll be a handful," Cage warned earlier that night. *"So, you gotta do this..."*

So far it appeared that Cage was right.

Catching him again, Ellis whipped out a gun and out of breath said, "Flow, stop running, nigga or we'll shoot."

Flow laughed. "My nigga, if Cage sent you, then you know that won't work."

"Look up, my guy," Shane said out of breath.

It was a full moon. Which meant that if he was shot or injured, he could die.

"Damn," Flow said, shaking his head. "It be your own people."

Fifteen minutes later, Flow was also locked away from the world, in a separate location from Bloom.

Angelina was gone.

He knew because she removed all of her clothes from the closet.

So now he hated her guts.

Normally when he woke up at night the first thing he did was grab a few more seconds of sleep because his body was so exhausted. But on this particular night, the moment the sun went down, he walked around their room.

Everything she owned was gone.

And then something happened that changed his mind.

Maybe she didn't leave that night.

A woman from an apartment complex called wondering why she hadn't shown up for her visit.

By T. Styles

And for reasons Cage couldn't guess, she put him down as a reference.

When he walked to the kitchen, Tatum was there waiting.

"I think something may be wrong with Angelina," Tatum said immediately.

Cage looked at his brother and said, "What you mean?"

"She didn't seem right yesterday. She seemed as if she was trying to tell me something but was afraid."

"Why would she tell you and not me?" Cage shrugged.

"I know you have your people; you may want to get them to go look for her."

Cage was already triggered by the real estate woman, so that's exactly what he did.

Sent a search party for her.

He combed the streets.

He went to her favorite restaurants.

In the end they all said the same thing.

That they hadn't seen her. He was growing restless and angry.

After coming up short, he went to his bed and threw his weight backward.

If something happened to her due to his beef with Onion, he would never forgive himself.

More than anything, at that moment, he didn't know what to do next.

Think Cage. Think.

Onion was at his home, looking at his supply of Vitamin D oil. After having his collection annihilated, he knew he had to go to the next step. And there were people who wanted to help.

"Bring her in," Onion said to Cheddar. "And then leave us alone."

Irritated, Cheddar went into the lobby and returned with Mink.

"Now go," Onion told him.

He shook his head and left.

"Do you have my boyfriend?"

"I don't know what you're talking about."

"I can't find my man," she cried to Onion. "And I want to know if you have him or not."

"Who is that?"

"Flow."

"Nah, the little nigga not here."

"Well, I need your help finding him."

Onion thought about what was happening. This situation might be exactly what he needed.

"Why should I help you?"

"I chose him. And in Wolf culture that's a serious thing. Without him, nobody in the pack would have me." She looked down. "I'm done."

"I don't have him, but I know where he may be. And I have a plan. But you have to get into Cage's house to execute it. Because he's probably there."

By T. Styles

Onion gave her details while also keeping an eye on her moves. He had no intentions on being a Wolf's dinner.

When he was done explaining he said, "Can you do this?"

"If you're sure, I'll do whatever I have to do."

"I need it done tonight."

"I'm ready."

After making love, Cage rolled over in the bed and looked Helena in the eyes. "This was always your plan wasn't it?"

She smiled. "Why does it have to be more than what I've already expressed?"

"Refresh my mind."

"Just like the others in the Stryker Collection I was born to protect you. And I'm going to do that no matter what. If protecting you means to see to it that you have peace then so be it. If it means you want the pussy then so be it. I'm not plotting. Because there is no need to plot."

"Nah..." Cage said. "You want to be queen."

She smiled. "If you want me to stand at your side I--."

"Stop playing fucking games and answer my question."

"Yes. I want it all."

He grinned.

Cage rolled over to get his phone, when out of the corner of his eye he saw a letter. Popping up to get it he read its contents.

Cage, I decided that I am not the woman you need me to be. I'm sorry.

Cage closed the note and tossed it on the table.

"Is everything okay?" She asked.

"Yes. Everything makes sense now. She didn't need the two weeks. She's gone for good."

Although he was crushed that she wasn't able to rise to the occasion, at least he knew she left of her own accord. Now it was time to plot out the next point of his life.

Without her.

So why was she still on his mind?

Suddenly there was a thundering banging on the door.

"Come in!"

"Sir, there is someone at the gate!" Langley said.

"Who is it?"

"I don't know her name. But she's a Wolf. I can smell her from here."

He frowned and grabbed his robe. "Let her in but keep an eye on her every move."

When Cage got dressed with Helena and ten of his collection following, he met Mink in the lobby.

"Who are you?"

She sniffed the air, unconsciously overwhelmed by the delicious odor of their bodies.

Flow was right.

The collection stood in front of Cage in protection mode, sensing something was off.

244

"What was that about?" Helena whispered to Cage, having seen her sniff the air.

He knew, but decided against telling any of them, for fear that knowing would cause an immediate war between Vamps and Wolves.

"What you doing here?"

"My name is Mink. And I'm here to tell you that your brother may be in trouble."

He frowned. "What are you talking about?"

"He's selling drugs with Onion."

"Even if I were to believe you, why you coming to me?"

"Because everyone says that you are in charge. That you haven't sat on your throne yet, but eventually you will. So, I need your help to get him back."

He knew what she didn't.

That it was Cage who held Flow hostage, not Onion.

As she spoke, Cage's Vamps began circling her.

Cage perceived something else was up and he was right.

Nodding his head once, they grabbed her and searched her body. It didn't take long for them to find the oil.

He smiled when he saw the label.

"Didn't even think to pull this off huh?"

She rolled her eyes. "What are you going to do with me?"

"Whatever I desire." He grinned.

Focusing on Langley and Helena he used his mind to say, "*Put part two of our plan into action.*"

Helena walked away to get up with the other members of the Stryker Collection leaving them alone.

Cheddar was in his home preparing his evening when suddenly he felt a chill up his spine. Walking out of his room, he wasn't surprised when he saw Helena and twenty others staring at him.

"I knew this day would come." He tightened his arms across his chest.

"Oh yeah, nigga?" Langley said.

"How did you know where I was?"

"We didn't," Helena smiled. "The Elders told us."

That's why he didn't fuck with they old asses. And if he survived, they would have words, he was certain.

"So, you gonna kill me?" He glared. "How? We bought up all the D. It ain't nowhere to be found."

Helena dipped into her pocket. "You mean this?"

His eyes widened. "How did you--"

"Onion gave this to a young Wolf tonight, in an attempt to kill Cage. But Cage is smarter. Then again you know that already."

Cheddar smiled and shook his head. "I knew this nigga Onion would get me killed one of these days."

"I guess you were right," Helena said.

Onion spent the next hour trying to find Cheddar.

Losing him would cripple him at the legs. So, he called all of his allies and not one of them was helpful.

With nowhere else to run he went to the last place on earth anyone would expect him to go.

There were only four hours left in the evening before Cage and his collection would have to settle down for the night. When all of a sudden Helena came running into his room.

"Onion is at the gate!"

"What you talking about?"

"He's here! He's really here!"

Cage's fangs dropped.

Onion was strapped to a chair in the ceremony room with all 50 of Cage's collection surrounding him. Although there were smiles planted on the members of his collection's faces, Cage knew something else was going on.

This was a chess move on Onion's part, he was certain.

Cage approached. "You look well fed, my nigga. Being in charge looks good on you."

"Why did you come here tonight?" He said calmly.

"You've been looking for me forever and this is what you ask? After I basically gift wrap myself for you?"

"What do you want?"

"You killed every member in the O collection." Now he was serious. "You even got Cheddar, don't you?"

Silence.

"The way it looks, I have no other tools in my arsenal. So that's why I came. To in a sense, put an end to it all."

"You sent somebody to my home tonight. To kill me."

"Because you left me no choice! We were friends and what did you do? Fuck and marry my bitch. You know how foul that is? I think about that shit every fucking night."

"You rewriting history. You killed my father. And then, because I wasn't aware of what you did, I gave you the opportunity to treat Angelina right. You failed. So, I took her back."

Onion grinned. "Is that still the case?" He leaned closer. "Is she still yours?"

By T. Styles

Caged knew at that moment that he was fully aware that his marriage was trash. "I'm still waiting on the real answer. Why are you here?"

"I want you to kill me."

Cage glared. "You a fucking liar."

"Why else would I turn myself over to you? So go on and kill me with my own D."

Cage looked over at Helena who gave him the bottle of oil the young Wolf brought to the house earlier that night. Twisting off the cap, he looked down at Onion.

"You mean this?" And with that he drank every drop.

Onion's eyes widened as he waited for him to die a painful death.

He was still standing.

"How are you...how are you able to do that?"

"All of the D in this area is fake." He tossed the bottle across the room. "Nothing more than avocado oil. I bought the company E&I Services months ago."

"Why?"

"Because years ago, I let out the secret of how to get rid of us. And I needed to make that right. For now. I'm sure they will be able to get it at some time, but not in this area. As you can see."

Cage smiled at the look of disappointment on his face. "So, if you bought it all up that means you have the real amounts."

"What you think, nigga?"

The Collection smiled proudly realizing that they were seeing their king at work.

"That's pretty good. But I have a few things up my sleeves too."

"I'm not surprised."

"I didn't just make an *O-Collection*. I made an *N-Collection*. I made an *I-Collection*. I made another *O2-Collection*. And I made another *N2-Collection*."

Cage was now aware that he made a collection for every letter in his name.

"In other words, there are 200 more members of my collection out there that you know nothing about. And when I show up missing they will be unleashed on this city and this world. No longer will blood in chalices be enough. They will take to the streets. They will take to necks. And we will blame you."

The Stryker Collection looked at one another, knowing this would be a problem.

"Why would you do that? Why bring down The Collective?"

"You stole the one thing I cared about. Isn't that enough?"

Cage hated him even more. "The thing is, you're going to unleash them, with or without me letting you go."

"True. But it doesn't matter much now does it?" Onion laughed.

"I'm still going to kill you. And then I will find every member and kill them too. At this point I have enough D to make it possible. You know why?"

"Tell me, my nigga."

"Because your people move by pussy, wine and blood. So, it'll be easy. You can't win."

Cage looked back at his collection and said, "Bring me a vial out of the safe."

As one of the members walked away Onion sighed. "Did you ever think it would come to this?"

"What you talking about now?" He was sick of this nigga.

"Did you ever think that when we were kids that this would be our story? Two Vampires, who were once friends, looking to take each other out over a woman." He laughed.

"You mean my wife?"

"Is she though?" He tilted his head to the left.

Cage shifted a little. "For someone about to die you sure are in a good mood."

"I have two other tricks up my sleeve I didn't tell you about."

"Meaning?"

"I have Angelina. Well, I don't actually *have* her, but I know where she is." He grinned.

Cage knew that was his bag, but he wondered how he would play his hand. "Don't play games with me."

"I would never play with you like this." He laughed. "I know where she is. and if I don't show up tomorrow night she will be in a lot of pain."

In Cage's heart, the moment he showed up at his mansion, he knew he had her, but if she wanted him what could he do?

Except kill his ass.

"A lot of pain? So, you would torture her?"

He glared. "I would never do that. But if you kill me, you will."

"I'm growing sick of you."

"She may be your wife, but she's in my collection. The N2-Collection actually. And if you kill me she will be in the most pain of her life due to me dying."

Now Cage wanted him dead twice.

"You converted her when you know what the fuck we go through living at night? Fuck is wrong with you?" He yelled. "Why would you do that!"

The pain Cage felt from hearing the news brought a few of his collection members to their knees. For he was in physical pain, which they experienced immediately.

Onion loved every minute of it. "You kill me, and she dies too."

"You got this, boss," Langley said with his mind. He was the first to get back on his feet. *"Don't let him fuck with you."*

Cage looked at Langley and stood up fully. Other members of the Stryker Collection did the same.

Onion caught this exchange between him and Langley and wondered what was happening.

"If I kill you, she will be in pain. But she'll survive."

"True. But what about the baby she's carrying?"

Cage trembled. "She's pregnant?"

Now it was Onion who hated him for not realizing. "And guess who told me that?" He smiled. "Flow, before you had him snatched. Said he went to dinner with her and that she couldn't drink wine. He figured the card he gave me would be a way to restore our relationship. But I still don't fuck with him."

"You sound ridiculous!"

"You know what I find ridiculous?" He yelled. "You had the nerve to condemn me for how I treated her! And yet you ignored her! You forced her to have to fuck you in the daytime while you were asleep. What kind of husband is that? But I'm the villain?"

She told him?

"I can't believe she's...she's pregnant." Cage said.

"The thing that makes this unique is with your baby being inside of her body and my fluid being in her veins we're sort of connected aren't we? And the strangest part about this all is no one has ever made

By T. Styles

a record of a baby surviving in the womb of a woman in the Fluid Line of a murdered master. To make this easier. I die. Your baby dies too, bitch."

"The hate I feel for you will be enough for me to see you die in the most painful way possible."

"Could be true." He shrugged. "But it won't be for the next nine months now will it?" He sighed. "Do me a favor, take these ropes off. My wrists hurt. Oh, and release Cheddar too and I'll set her free." He winked.

Cage released him.

And had him followed.

But in preparation, all two hundred members of his collection were instructed to come out of hiding, and they were waiting on Onion's arrival at home.

Still, just as Onion stated, within ten minutes of Cage's release, Angelina was back at the crib.

And although he finally knew where Onion lived, he was 100% certain that by tomorrow night he would be gone.

Never to be found unless he desired.

He was right.

Returning home, the moment Cage saw Angelina the first thing he recognized was that the smell of fruit that once covered her body was replaced with rain.

His body tightened. "You disgust me."

She was already crying. "Onion took me and--"

"Don't lie! I know you went to him to be converted. I read it in the letter."

"I didn't write that in the letter." She frowned.

"I read between the lines. You knew I would never convert you, so you went behind my back and not only used me to get pregnant but allowed him to bite you. And I'm sure you gave him your body too, didn't you?"

"I did ask him to turn me. At first he wouldn't but all of a sudden, he called me to say he changed his mind." She sniffled.

"That's because he knew you were pregnant."

"I had a feeling I might be but when I took a pregnancy test it read '*Not Positive*'. So when Onion called to say he would convert me, after saying no, I came over. When I got there he made me take another one. It was positive and I tried to leave but he wouldn't let me go. That's when he converted me anyway! I even tried to come back home after it was done, but they still wouldn't let me leave. All I wanted was to fight for my marriage."

"What did you offer him in return?"

Silence.

"What did you give him?"

"Cage, I'm so sorry."

"You've done more damage than I can ever forgive." He walked away and she followed. "When my baby is born I want you out."

"Cage, we can make this work. I'm pregnant with your child so we have to make this work. You have to talk to me!"

He opened the bedroom door and Helena was inside waiting for him.

Angelina's legs buckled.

254   By T. Styles

He slammed the door in her face.

Angelina went to one of the many guest rooms in the house and pulled the blinds open. There wasn't much time before the sun rose and she was determined to kill herself by sunlight.

In her mind if Cage didn't want her why should she care?

What was the purpose of living?

But the closer it got to the sun rising she was exhausted. In a way she never felt before. She fought with nature to remain awake, but her body was no longer her own. And as a result, she shut down minutes before sunrise.

Slamming down to the floor, out of the rays of sunlight, it was now a fact that Angelina was a Vampire.

Cheddar and Onion were driving to an apartment building in Philadelphia. Onion hated giving him props, but he had to admit that Cheddar was smart.

Onion wanted him around not only because of the information he possessed. But also, because he was determined to be as smart as he was in the future. In the end he would take over his suave way of being so he could get what he wanted too.

"Thank you for making me create the other collection members," Onion said. "You should have seen the look on Cage's face when I told him we had 200."

"I'm glad you listened."

"So where we going?"

"You'll see."

Fifteen minutes later they were allowed inside a building, and then the only apartment on the lower level.

A man wearing a beanie greeted Cheddar and nodded. They both were allowed inside.

Sitting on a recliner was Anderson.

He was one thousand years old but looked every bit of thirty-five. His skin was vanilla, and his eyes were like caramel candies.

"Thank you for meeting with me," Cheddar said. "Please tell my friend what you told me earlier."

"Do you think he's ready?"

"Things are about to happen between the Wolves and Vamps. We have no choice."

"What's this about?" Onion asked, too antsy to fall back and wait.

Anderson explained everything to Onion. About the purpose of Vampires. And how the Wolves are put on earth for population control. Which is why they are awakening to Vampire flesh.

256   By T. Styles

But what he said next let Onion know the severity.

"Every few hundred years the Vampires are supposed to succumb to the plan. To be eaten by Wolves. To keep the number of Vampires under control."

"I don't get it." Onion shrugged.

"The Elders, people like me, have made an unwritten pact to sacrifice a portion of the Vampire population to the Wolfpack. This prevents a war. The way it should work is Elders first, those two hundred years and older. This cycle should continue. But lately, this group of Elders refuse to make the sacrifice. Instead, they work to manipulate young Vampires to kill themselves."

Onion was livid.

"In order for this to happen, you need to find a Vampire of honor, who believes in the bigger plan. This Vampire is usually respected. And can garner the respect of the younger Vampires too. He often has suffered a great loss and this loss fuels his guilt which leads him to sacrifice. We know that the time has come when the Wolves crave our flesh. That time is now."

"Why are you still alive?" Onion asked. "Shouldn't you be sacrificed too, nigga?"

"I wanted to die. Do you know what it's like to lose people you love? But I can't go until the Elders do what was planned. And since they have Tino's son, who's charismatic, it won't happen any time soon."

Cheddar looked at Onion. "So, basically they using Cage's dumb ass and shit is about to get crazy."

Arabia was in her home preparing to go to sleep when there was a knock at her door. Before she could open it someone allowed themself inside.

It was Helena and several members of the Stryker Collection.

"So, this is what Cage does now? Force himself into my home just because I won't answer the phone?"

"He wants to see you. And you're coming with us."

"How did you get in? Without an invitation."

"He made you say we are welcome at the ceremony. You were confused. But he was planning in advance because he never trusted your ass."

She shook her head and smiled.

He was smarter than she thought.

"Give me a few minutes to get dressed."

"You got two." Helena said.

Once at Cage's Mansion, Arabia met with him alone in the lounge. "What's with the moving boxes?"

"Can't stay here anymore." Cage smiled. "It's time to bounce."

"Well, I see you're embracing your use of power. Why trick me into giving your collection an invitation?"

"Because I don't trust you." He moved closer.

"Cage, just because I didn't agree with you, doesn't mean I—"

"Who is Viking?"

By T. Styles

She trembled. "He's...he's—"

"Before you answer, move as if I already know because I do."

She swallowed the lump in her throat. "He's..."

"Your lover. Your man. And he's also an Elder."

She shivered. "You can't violate my privacy."

"I can do whatever I so desire! And you left me no choice. You wouldn't answer my calls. So, I had to find out why."

"There was no need to do all of that. I made clear where I stand on your revenge plan. I wanted no parts of it. I want no parts of it now."

"So, you run away from the war? Just because you don't like the battle plan? That's childish."

The way he spoke to her let her know whether he knew it or not he was shaping himself into a king.

"What do you want with me?"

"I want you. By my side. Onion has made some moves that I'm concerned about for the future."

"Why should I help you?"

"You don't spend the majority of your life helping me take my position at the throne just to abandon me when I'm ready. Will you help me?"

Arabia knew there was no way she could sit by on the sidelines and allow the many things that were about to happen to go down without her assistance. Especially if she could do something about it.

And so, she agreed.

"If I help you, you must take my advice to heart. No more making major decisions without me."

"If you stay at my side I will always listen to you. I will take into full account what you suggest. But understand this, I am in charge. And my decisions, even if you don't like them, are my decisions all the same. You will learn to respect that. And never betray me by leaving me again."

She smiled. "I see you now."

"What is your response?"

"I agree."

"Good because we have major problems. Onion has turned over about 200 members of his collection. Including my wife."

Her head lowered. "This is the worst of everything you said to me."

"Why?"

"She's an addict. And as I've mentioned many times before, the taste of blood when you acquire it naturally from a human source gives a higher sensation than any drug could."

"You didn't tell me that."

"Oh, I'm sorry. I thought I did."

Cage readjusted. "Are you hiding anything else from me? Because if I find out you are, it will end badly for you."

"That was a mishap on my part."

"Make that the end of the things you choose to forget."

She swallowed. "You're right. Um...I...in reference to Angelina, I don't have to tell you because you know already, that she's an addict who hasn't dealt with her illness. This will cause major problems for you. And for us."

"Go deeper."

"She could end up being more vicious and eviller than any Vampire who has ever existed."

"What can I do?"

"Is she here?"

"Yes."

"Kill her."

By T. Styles

"I can't."

"Why?"

"She's pregnant."

"Would you have if she wasn't?"

Silence.

"For now, we'll keep an eye on her," Arabia said. "But if she survives, expect hell on earth."

"Understood. Now what do I do about the 200? I have some ideas but I need more."

"I heard that one of the Elders told you where Cheddar was. Which one is it?"

"I prefer not to say. Per his request."

She was slightly uncomfortable.

This Elder, whoever he was, now had direct access to the king.

"Well, having a relationship with the Elders means you have thousands in this area alone who are willing to help when the time comes. I've invited the best in the strongest over here now. I made the call when your collection came to get me. They're out in your backyard waiting to meet you."

Cage walked to his window and sure enough they covered the lawn. It looked to be about 400 of the most beautiful people he'd ever seen in his life. And although they were called Elders their faces were as young as his own.

"I didn't think they would look so young."

"No one ever does."

"Do you know why I keep you around?"

"Because I'm useful?" She smiled.

"True. And the moment you stop being, you will cease to exist." He placed a heavy hand on her shoulder and squeezed. It hurt. "Are you ready?"

Tatum stood in the mirror getting dressed. When his door opened and he saw Cage walk inside, he took a deep breath.

"Do you know where Bloom and Flow are, brother?"

"I don't," Cage lied. "But I'm sure they're fine. Right now, we have to focus on you." He took a deep breath.

"How can the uncles be sure this will work? The pack didn't even notice me at first. All of their attention was on Flow."

"When you walked into that room that night, and it was time to meet them, how did you act?"

"I can't remember."

"Did you walk with your head held high? Did you feel like you deserved to be in the room? Did you demand respect based on being Magnus' son alone?"

"No. Not even close." He laughed once.

"Well Flow did. And that's what they detected. Tonight, when you meet with them that will change."

"How do you know I can do this?"

"I've watched you amass over ten million subscribers on your social media accounts. People look up to you. Many of them are Wolves and they don't even know who you are. Command that same presence tonight. And they will follow you. I will follow you too."

By T. Styles

Later on, that night, with Cage in the back room and the uncles on the podium, everyone awaited Tatum's arrival.

Just as it happened many times before, the uncles were able to demand moments of respect but for the most part the younger Wolves were rowdy, loud, and mad disrespectful.

To be honest the uncles didn't think Tatum had what it took to command a room, but Cage thought otherwise.

So, they decided to trust him.

A few seconds later Tatum walked inside.

And instead of moving toward the podium and avoiding eye contact he looked at every last Wolf in the eyes.

He was strong.

He was confident.

Every Wolf in the room paused.

Even the uncles.

This was a first.

"They think we're animals!" Tatum yelled from the floor. "They say we don't have an identity. That we follow the Vampires because we hate who we are and we think they're better. And you're proving them right! I am not an animal. I am a descendant of the most powerful species on earth. I am WOLF and so are you!" He beat his chest and his muscles popped.

The crowd went the fuck off.

This was the vibe they needed.

"Today, everything they think they know about us will change! You either get with the program, or face consequences. Are you ready?"

The room cheered.

The uncles were proud.

"Now, before we get into some pack shit..." he looked at Gunnar. "Get this traitor and his muts the fuck out of here. They dead to us!"

On his word, Gunnar and his people were tossed out on the street.

For now, order was restored.

Cage walked outside to make a phone call. It rang once before he finally answered.

"Where do you live now?" Cage asked Onion.

Onion laughed. "Now I know you didn't think it would be that easy."

"It was worth a try."

"What do you want?"

"You said you had two tricks up your sleeves. Judging by the smile on your face when I saw you, I could tell you wanted me to know the second one. So, what is it?"

"What if I tell you that all of our steps are ordered. Or outlined?"

"I'm confused."

"What if I told you that there's somebody writing our journey. In a book. And that person controls the people we meet. The situations that happen to us. Even if we live or die. And that I can get access to that person. Would you believe me?"

"Are you talking about God?"

"In a manner of speaking."

264   By T. Styles

"I would call you crazy."

"And that would be your biggest mistake."

Fisher stood in the kitchen of his restaurant.

Instead of preparing a meal, he was preparing a wine and blood mixture that he was certain would be a hit with Vampires. Who, although they didn't eat food, were growing tired of not having enough blood variety and wine.

When he heard the bell ring on the door he yelled, "Sit where you want! I'll be right there!"

"Hurry, handsome," Helena said. "Don't keep me waiting too long."

Within five minutes Fisher walked out holding two golden chalices. Before walking over, he looked at Helena who sat under the only chandelier lit. The majority of the restaurant was dark.

Wearing a white tank top with a gold necklace that read Helena, he smiled.

"Why are you so fucking sexy?"

"Are you going to join me?" She whipped her hair over her shoulder and crossed her legs.

He walked in her direction, placed the two chalices down and said, "Wait...I have to play some music first."

Within a minute of his disappearance, the song, A Muse by DVSN played softly on the speakers.

Quickly he returned and sat in front of her. "Please say you haven't tasted it yet."

"Of course I didn't." She smiled and reached over and touched his hand. "I was waiting for you." She squeezed lightly. "Now, what's in it?"

"Herbs we can taste, a variation of several wines and of course, sweet blood."

"Sounds yummy. You know me so well."

"Of course, I do. We've been dating for--."

"One month." She winked. "And it was worth every moment."

CAGE'S NEW MANSION

When Angelina awoke, from her Vampire sleep, she was shocked to see Cage sitting on a chair in her room. Because he hadn't said a word to her since she was converted, she shivered.

"I can't believe that sweet smell, that exotic odor that I loved about you, has turned to rain."

"What are you...what are you doing inside here?"

She hoped he was there to get back together, to repair their marriage, but she also believed that Helena, who shared his bed some nights, wanted him.

"I'm ready to talk to you."

She nodded. "O...okay."

"This shit, this person I am now, is different from who you knew before." His words came out heavy.

By T. Styles

Like they were the truest and most painful things he ever said. "And I guess, I guess I ain't want to hear you say it wasn't me. Because if it's not me, then it wasn't you. And I needed what we had to be the one thing that remained the same."

"Cage, I'm—."

He raised his hand, silencing her instantly. "But you know what, sometimes in life you gotta be the villain. So I'm good on that shit now." He nodded.

She trembled with fear.

"When you first met Onion, why didn't you get with him then?"

"Cage, I really don't--."

"I'm just asking, baby," he said sweetly.

He hadn't called her baby in a while, so she softened immediately. And still, his mix bag of emotions let her know something was coming. "Because I...I felt him and it was too strong."

"Go deeper."

"He...he wanted me so badly that I was afraid that if things didn't go right, if I did the slightest thing wrong, that he would...that he would hurt me."

He nodded. "And you didn't get that impression with me?"

She shook her head no.

"Big mistake."

"Cage, what's going on?"

"Over this past month, it's been hell, baby." He closed his hands and squeezed them so tightly together she thought they would crack. "Every night...every fucking night I go to a place so dark in my mind, that I lose myself. And in this place I imagine you kissing him. Touching him. And fucking him."

"Please, Cage. I don't want Onion. If I wanted him I could—."

"Have him? I know." He bit his bottom lip. "If you wanted him you could have him. Cause you always had the power right between your fucking legs didn't you? Since we were kids. But let me ask you something?"

"Anything."

"What kind of woman that make you? A whore?"

Suddenly her stomach hurt badly, and she doubled over in pain.

"Do you remember me telling you how much pain I was in, after JoJo drank the D and died? In that restaurant?"

She grabbed her head and her stomach. "What's...what's happening? I think I'm having a miscarriage."

"Do you remember or not?"

"Yes." She cried as agony ripped through her body.

"Well you are about to experience that too."

"So you...so you killed Onion?" She asked with wide eyes that turned red due to the distress she was under.

"Onion has done a good job of hiding. So for now he's safe. But I found one of the forty-nine assistants that helped in your conversion. And right now, in a restaurant, he's drinking blood tainted with D."

She fell to her knees.

He rose.

"There is good news and bad news. The pain you're in won't be as excruciating as it would be if Onion died, since he's your fucking master. But you won't know it because it will be the most painful night of your life."

268

"Cage, I'm hurting."

"I warned you. I told you not to cross me and you did it anyway."

"Cage, no...you...why would you do this! I'm pregnant!"

"Did you actually think I would allow you to have my baby? When you're a member of that nigga's line?" He trembled so hard it looked as if he were about to explode. "You are dead to me, Angelina."

On his way out of the room, as she experienced the pain of someone in her line dying, she looked at him with hate.

"I will remember this," she cried. "And I will make you pay."

He shrugged. "Fuck the future. Focus on now. It's about to be a long ass night, mommy."

He slammed the door, and she screamed out in pain.

1 YEAR LATER

A half-moon sat high over a scenic wooden gazebo in the center of a luscious thick forest. Crickets and owls worked the background vocals for what promised to be an epic fucking night.

In the middle of it all, Angelina sat on a black velvet and gold king's chair, with 68 members of her collection standing behind her. Her right hand, the 69th, stood beside her.

All women.

All Vampires.

All deadly.

Wearing a red lace catsuit, which showed her small brown nipples and landing strip leading to her pussy, she widened her legs. Looking to her right, a thug ass nigga from East Baltimore crawled in her direction. Sitting on his knees, he leaned toward her, nestling his chest between her warm pussy.

With her hand on the top of his head, she yanked to the right, exposing the jugular.

Yeah...that's nice.

Quickly she bit down into him and sucked hard. And long. Angelina only drank from the source.

No cup.

No straw.

Just skin and blood.

The blood sucking sensation was so powerful that the pressure his weakening body placed on her clit caused her to reach a private orgasm. When she felt him falling too soon, she wrapped her leg around his back and pulled him closer.

Her red toenails wiggled with delight.

When he was half empty, she allowed him to drop to the ground as her 68 drug him away.

They could have the rest.

Looking up at Carmen, the sole member of Onion's first collection, she said, "Will they be on time?" She whipped her long hair over her shoulder. Since becoming a Vampire her skin had freshened and she looked as young as she did when she was a teenager.

By T. Styles

Carmen might not have been of her fluid, but Angelina still considered her an honorary member of her collection.

"Yes, my queen." Carmen wiped the blood off the corner of her master's lips. "I believe they will."

"If this doesn't work, I will blame you." She licked her mouth.

Carmen took a deep breath. "I know. And I may do many things in life but letting you down won't be one of them."

Angelina winked.

As they waited on their guests, Angelina thought about her circumstances. One year ago to the day, a man she thought loved her left her in excruciating pain, in a room at his new mansion.

Due to a member in her line being killed.

She didn't trust him.

She didn't trust any men.

And so, as he bedded his new whore, she crawled out the window.

Luckily for her, Carmen, who vowed to seek revenge on Cage, due to being rejected from being in his collection, was dating a member of the Stryker Collection to plot her plan. After many months of laying low at his house, she was eventually able to follow him to Cage's new mansion undetected.

And on that exact day, she saw Angelina crawling on the grass in pain.

Kismet?

Maybe.

Not believing her eyes, she blew her cover and rushed in her direction. Helping her to her car, she drove her from the scene.

Tucked in Carmen's small home, she nursed Angelina back to health. It was a long hard road, but in the end, it was the best thing she had ever done.

Because Angelina lived up to the hype.

First, she united the female Vampires, who were abandoned by the men they loved. When word got out about the rogue female master who was bringing women together, in the name of revenge, some left their collections to assist her efforts.

This gave her the 49 needed to convert her own collection.

All while Cage and Onion tried to find her whereabouts.

But who would join the collection of a woman who some said was bitter due to her man choosing another?

Many.

Woman after woman came to her with the same stories. Of how their men left them because although they had the gene, they weren't Vampires. Every female, every single one, lost their man to a member within their own collection.

Angelina's squad, you could call them bitter but they wouldn't give a fuck, became the most vicious Vampire gang ever.

They were known as The Lina's.

She preferred the 69.

And now they were moving to the next level of Angelina's plan.

Within seconds, they heard rustling of branches in the distance. Small animals scurried away.

Angelina inhaled the air. "They're here."

Led by Mink, twenty female Wolves who were exiled due to their men leaving them, dying or simply choosing another, strolled in Angelina's direction.

272

Thick, juicy and beautiful, the Wolves exuded power which was Angelina's brand.

Under the moonlight, the Wolves stopped short of walking into the gazebo.

It felt like a sacred place.

"I didn't think you would come." Angelina said with her head raised high.

"We're sick of the games too." Mink shrugged. "So why not see what's good?"

Angelina rose slowly from her chair and walked toward them. Her bare feet cracked small broken branches and pressed against the damp earth as she moved closer.

The 69 followed.

Standing before Mink, Angelina said, "Tell me your story, Wolf."

Mink sighed. "Your lover, the king."

"He's no king of mine!" Angelina said, deading that shit with the quickness.

Mink nodded. "I have reason to believe that Cage took Flow from me. He was the Wolf I'd chosen. And when I returned to the pack for support, and even for hopes of a future, I was made to believe that although they may fuck me, my honor was destroyed without him. No other Wolf would take me as their wife leaving me virtually alone. And I'm sick of these antiquated ass policies!"

The Wolves cheered.

"Since they won't change, we will no longer be a part of their games." Mink continued. "And there are plenty more who will follow me if you desire."

Angelina looked back at the 69 and back at Mink. "Carmen tells me Cage had you in his home. How did you escape?"

She sighed. "I saw my life flash before my eyes that night. They were going to kill me. Due to my attempt to poison Cage. But something must've happened to Cage for a moment, because all of a sudden, the Vamps holding me dropped to their knees. I was able to overpower them in that brief second and escape."

Angelina smiled.

She approved.

"The Wolves are awakening to their cravings."

"True."

"How can I trust you?"

Mink laughed. "I can't lie, y'all smell good as fuck to me." She inhaled deeply.

The 69 got ready to attack.

Angelina was without fear and so she raised her hand, preventing the fight.

"But none of my people here tonight tasted Vamp flesh. And the pain..." she took a deep breath. "No, scratch that, the rage I feel against my own is far more than enough to stop my craving for you, beautiful."

Angelina nodded.

"So, queen, what is your plan?" Mink asked, as the exiled female Wolves moved closer. "How will you unite us?"

"We will start by wreaking havoc on the city, and letting the world know we exist, and that we ain't going nowhere."

They cheered.

"And then?"

"We kill Cage." Angelina continued, as her fangs dropped. "And Onion."

It was a bit on the nose, but the female Wolves howled in excitement.

Fang's dropped, The Lina's cheered.

PRESENT DAY
"It's your freedom."

When Violet awakened after taking a long nap which lasted into the evening she was shocked to smell the scent of herbs and spices in her home.

Had she left something on?

She couldn't be sure.

Pulling herself up off the sofa which was her new resting place she walked to the kitchen. Only to see Pierre preparing a meal.

She smiled. "You know I can get used to this."

"Word?"

She giggled. "I'm serious. I love seeing you here."

"It's been weeks. You aren't tired of me yet?"

"Never." She stepped closer. "What are you making?"

"I have some red beans and rice soup. It's a recipe from one of my favorite chefs. Dom Yum Yum."

"Well, it smells delicious, and I can't wait to eat some."

"I also have something else for you."

"A home-cooked meal and a gift? This is heaven on earth."

He walked up to her and softly took her hand. After helping her get dressed into a sweat suit, he walked her to his car where they were driven to a huge body of land. The moment she saw the rolling hills and corn, she knew exactly where they were.

"Violet, you mentioned you did something that you were ashamed of. Something you couldn't take back. What was it?"

She looked at the beautiful land. "I...I don't want to ruin the moment."

"You can't ruin anything with me." He looked a bit harder. "So talk to me."

She took a deep breath. "One day I ran into my aunt at the grocery store. She was estranged from the family."

"What else happened?"

"She...my aunt...she's my grandmother's daughter. And she was pregnant with a son, and I knew she was running from something. She was afraid. She needed to find her mother. And I...I told her...I told her I didn't know where my grandmother was even though I was on my way to see her that night. Basically, I lied and claimed I couldn't help her." She sighed. "She died and I think my grandmother felt guilty."

He smiled. "My, Sweet Violet, you shouldn't take on the responsibility for something like that."

"You don't know what it feels like."

"I have done worse."

"Really?"

Silence.

She redirected her attention to the acres of land and remembered. "This is where you grew up?" She asked. "From the story you told me in the coffee shop?"

He smiled.

"It's beautiful, Pierre."

"Come with me. I want to show you a few things."

After walking her to a body of grass she looked down and saw what appeared to be two unmarked graves.

"What is this?"

"It's your freedom." He said looking down at her. "You no longer have to be afraid of anyone. No one will threaten you anymore. No one will force you to do anything that you don't want. At the end of the day, you will be free to live, dream and create in peace."

She looked up at him in fear at first and then there was a sudden calmness over her body. A calm that bothered her greatly.

"Are these my..."

"Yes."

There was a silence between them that lasted long.

But Violet broke it after giving him a big hug.

If he did this he cared.

He really cared!

Besides, no one had ever given her such a gift. And although she should be afraid for so many reasons, she was comforted.

Her sisters were no more.

She was safe.

And so, she smiled.

Was she now the villain in her own story?

"This is the best thing anyone has ever done for me. And although I shouldn't be grateful I am. Why would you do this?"

"Because I want you to be happy. And I want you to be free to live out your grandmother's dreams when she eventually dies."

She frowned. "You mean the book?"

"Yes. You have to honor her by completing the story. You have to write the saga. And if you would allow me, I would love to help."

Coming January 2022

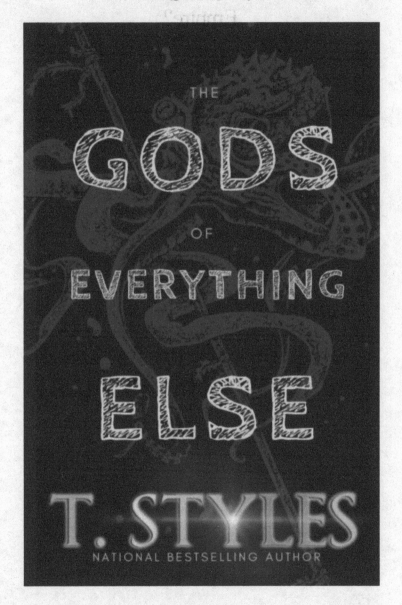

Are you looking to build your Book Empire?

Do you Need Help?

Visit:
www.theelitewritersacademy.com

For Planners, Courses and Templates

By T. Styles

CARTEL PUBLICATIONS

PRESENTS

The Cartel Publications Order Form

Shyt List 1	_____	$15.00
Shyt List 2	_____	$15.00
Shyt List 3	_____	$15.00
Shyt List 4	_____	$15.00
Shyt List 5	_____	$15.00
Shyt List 6	_____	$15.00
Pitbulls In A Skirt	_____	$15.00
Pitbulls In A Skirt 2	_____	$15.00
Pitbulls In A Skirt 3	_____	$15.00
Pitbulls In A Skirt 4	_____	$15.00
Pitbulls In A Skirt 5	_____	$15.00
Victoria's Secret	_____	$15.00
Poison 1	_____	$15.00
Poison 2	_____	$15.00
Hell Razor Honeys	_____	$15.00
Hell Razor Honeys 2	_____	$15.00
A Hustler's Son	_____	$15.00
A Hustler's Son 2	_____	$15.00
Black and Ugly	_____	$15.00
Black and Ugly As Ever	_____	$15.00
Ms Wayne & The Queens of DC **(LGBT)**	_____	$15.00
Black And The Ugliest	_____	$15.00
Year Of The Crackmom	_____	$15.00
Deadheads	_____	$15.00
The Face That Launched A Thousand Bullets	_____	$15.00
The Unusual Suspects	_____	$15.00
Paid In Blood	_____	$15.00
Raunchy	_____	$15.00
Raunchy 2	_____	$15.00
Raunchy 3	_____	$15.00
Mad Maxxx (4th Book Raunchy Series)	_____	$15.00
Quita's Dayscare Center	_____	$15.00

TREASON 2

Quita's Dayscare Center 2	_____	$15.00
Pretty Kings	_____	$15.00
Pretty Kings 2	_____	$15.00
Pretty Kings 3	_____	$15.00
Pretty Kings 4	_____	$15.00
Silence Of The Nine	_____	$15.00
Silence Of The Nine 2	_____	$15.00
Silence Of The Nine 3	_____	$15.00
Prison Throne	_____	$15.00
Drunk & Hot Girls	_____	$15.00
Hersband Material **(LGBT)** _	_____	$15.00
The End: How To Write A	_____	$15.00
Bestselling Novel In 30 Days (Non-Fiction Guide)		
Upscale Kittens	_____	$15.00
Wake & Bake Boys	_____	$15.00
Young & Dumb	_____	$15.00
Young & Dumb 2: Vyce's Getback	_____	$15.00
Tranny 911 **(LGBT)**	_____	$15.00
Tranny 911: Dixie's Rise **(LGBT)**	_____	$15.00
First Comes Love, Then Comes Murder	_____	$15.00
Luxury Tax	_____	$15.00
The Lying King	_____	$15.00
Crazy Kind Of Love	_____	$15.00
Goon	_____	$15.00
And They Call Me God	_____	$15.00
The Ungrateful Bastards	_____	$15.00
Lipstick Dom **(LGBT)**	_____	$15.00
A School of Dolls **(LGBT)**	_____	$15.00
Hoetic Justice	_____	$15.00
KALI: Raunchy Relived	_____	$15.00
(5th Book in Raunchy Series)		
Skeezers	_____	$15.00
Skeezers 2	_____	$15.00
You Kissed Me, Now I Own You	_____	$15.00
Nefarious	_____	$15.00
Redbone 3: The Rise of The Fold	_____	$15.00
The Fold (4th Redbone Book)	_____	$15.00
Clown Niggas	_____	$15.00
The One You Shouldn't Trust	_____	$15.00
The WHORE The Wind		
Blew My Way	_____	$15.00
She Brings The Worst Kind	_____	$15.00
The House That Crack Built	_____	$15.00
The House That Crack Built 2	_____	$15.00
The House That Crack Built 3	_____	$15.00
The House That Crack Built 4	_____	$15.00
Level Up **(LGBT)**	_____	$15.00
Villains: It's Savage Season	_____	$15.00
Gay For My Bae	_____	$15.00
War	_____	$15.00

By T. Styles

War 2: All Hell Breaks Loose _____	$15.00
War 3: The Land Of The Lou's _____	$15.00
War 4: Skull Island _____	$15.00
War 5: Karma _____	$15.00
War 6: Envy _____	$15.00
War 7: Pink Cotton _____	$15.00
Madjesty vs. Jayden (Novella) _____	$8.99
You Left Me No Choice _____	$15.00
Truce – A War Saga (War 8) _____	$15.00
Ask The Streets For Mercy _____	$15.00
Truce 2 - (War 9) _____	$15.00
An Ace and Walid Very, Very Bad Christmas (War 10) ____	$15.00
Truce 3 – The Sins of The Fathers (War 11) _____	$15.00
Truce 4: The Finale (War 12) _____	$15.00
Treason _____	$20.00
Treason 2 _____	$20.00

(**Redbone 1** & **2** are **NOT** Cartel Publications novels and if <u>ordered</u> the cost is **FULL** price of $15.00 **each**. <u>No Exceptions</u>.)

Please add **$7.00** for shipping and handling fees for up to **(2) BOOKS PER ORDER**. (INMATES INCLUDED) (See next page for details)

The Cartel Publications * P.O. BOX 486 OWINGS MILLS MD 21117

Name: _____

Address: _____

City/State: _____

Contact/Email: _____

Please allow 10-15 BUSINESS days Before shipping.

PLEASE NOTE DUE TO <u>COVID-19</u> SOME ORDERS MAY TAKE UP TO <u>3 WEEKS OR LONGER</u> BEFORE THEY SHIP

The Cartel Publications is <u>NOT</u> responsible for <u>Prison Orders</u> rejected!

TREASON 2   283

By T. Styles

CPSIA information can be obtained
at www.ICGtesting.com
Printed in the USA
LVHW101549200322
713908LV00012B/1657